Taggart's Crossing

John Taggart and Jacob Stuckey are Civil War veterans who operate a ferry on the mighty Arkansas River. When two drifters pick on Jacob, Taggart ruthlessly disarms them and sends them on their way as they vow revenge. But there is more trouble to come. Russ Decker and his gang steal a fortune in gold 'Double Eagles' from a bank in Wichita. Their escape route into the Indian Territories takes them by way of the ferry crossing. With a posse of Pinkerton Agents on their trail, they decide to stop the pursuit by putting John and Jacob out of business . . . permanently.

Unknown to Decker and his men, a Deputy US Marshal also has his sights on them, but the lawman first has to deliver a particularly unpleasant prisoner to Fort Smith. In addition to all this, fate decrees that a keelboat full of stolen silver ore will arrive at Taggart's Crossing just at the right moment to ensure maximum havoc.

By the same author

Blood On The Land
The Devil's Work
The Iron Horse
Pistolero
The Lawmen
The Outlaw Trail
Terror In Tombstone
The Deadly Shadow
Gone West
A Return To The Alamo

Taggart's Crossing

Paul Bedford

A Black Horse Western

ROBERT HALE

ISBN 978-0-7198-2156-1

The Crowood Press
The Stable Block
Crowood Lane
Ramsbury
Marlborough
Wiltshire SN8 2HR

www.bhwesterns.com

Robert Hale is an imprint
of The Crowood Press

*In fond memory of my father, Ronald (1924–1994).
I think he would have enjoyed this book.*

Typeset by
Derek Doyle & Associates, Shaw Heath
Printed and bound in Great Britain by
CPI Group (UK) Ltd, Croydon, CR0 4YY

CHAPTER ONE

'How the hell can four of us crew that thing?' Naylor demanded as he stared in wide-eyed shock at the big keelboat – also known as a poleboat, on account of the long wooden poles that were used for steering and to propel it upstream. 'It must need ten times our number.'

The black-haired monster of a man at his shoulder regarded him pityingly. 'Because we're only going *down* river, you simple shit. We'll have the current with us, not agin us. All we'll have to do is steal it and steer it.'

Darkness had finally fallen over Canon City, Colorado. Like most frontier mining camps it had its charms, *if* one had the ready cash to pay for them. Unfortunately for Ed Teach and his three cronies, nothing ever seemed to pan out quite the way it should. They had arrived at the diggings too late to secure a decent claim. Those already there were organized and proof against the petty theft and poorly planned violence which was Teach's usual *modus operandi.* Their faces had become known and their days numbered. It was time to pull off something spectacular and hightail it before they all ended up stretching a rope.

It was Teach, in his often shaky capacity as gang leader, who conveniently overheard a drunken conversation that seemed to offer the prospect of real gain. Because the railhead of the Denver and Rio Grande Railroad hadn't yet reached Canon City, the silver mined by the big operators had to be transported a distance of about a mile by road; the wagons were always heavily guarded, but a flash flood had just washed away the dirt track and so for a short while the valuable ore would be moved to the railhead by river. The precious cargos were still guarded, of course, but someone had decided that since the country's main arteries now consisted of railroads rather than rivers so the days of the river pirates must have passed. Consequently, the fifty-foot keelboat was already loaded ready for an early morning start, but only three poorly paid men patrolled the landing stage.

As the last rays of light had drained out of the sky, pitch torches had been lit, but the flaming light only illuminated the immediate area. Teach and his men were free to make their preparations unhindered. Hidden in a stand of Bristlecone Pine trees, the three ruffians watched with amazement as their boss produced a bottle of 'rot gut' from his jacket. He was not normally known for his generosity.

'What I need,' he announced in unusually hushed

tones, 'Is someone looking like they're on a ten-day drunk, who can distract those fellas for a moment. *And* you get to keep this bottle of Who Hit John. Who will it be?'

A twitchy, squinty-eyed character going by the colourful name of Barf Baxter immediately stuck his hand up. 'Me, me. I can do it, boss. I've been drunk most of my damn life. It'll be a piece of piss!'

Teach stared at him intently for a long moment. 'Fair enough, just don't mess up,' he finally replied. Menace coated every word and the other two men were suddenly glad it wasn't to be them. 'And hand over that belt gun,' he added. 'I don't want anything making them nervous.'

Accepting the well-worn Colt, the brutalized thug glanced at the other two. 'An' when we rush 'em, there's to be no shooting. You hear?'

Their shift had barely started and already the three guards were bored stiff. The enclosed cabin on the moored keelboat was a tempting resting place and maybe later, in the silent early hours, they would risk it. But for the time being they would prowl around and make a show of doing what they were paid for. After all, it was highly unlikely that they would actually be called upon to do anything dangerous.

A sudden commotion off in the dark had them reaching for their weapons, until a tremendous belch followed by a fit of giggling reassured them. Some miner had drunk far more than his fill and would doubtless regret it in the morning.

Baxter's unkempt figure swayed into view. He had made a sizeable dent in the cheap whiskey, just in case Teach might later change his mind, he had also poured some of it over his clothes for the sake of realism. His natural condition was to be unwashed and lice-ridden, so the resulting stench was overwhelming. As though suddenly spotting the three men, he waved gleefully at them and called out, 'Well howdy there, fellas. Ain't it purdy down by the river?'

One of the guards made a half-hearted attempt to warn him off, but in truth the man was glad of a diversion.

'Aw hell, mister,' Baxter protested loudly. 'I don't mean you no harm. Here, have a sip of this bug juice. It'll make you feel real good inside.' So saying, he tottered nearer with his hand outstretched.

The three sentries unsuspectingly closed in around him. They were sorely tempted to accept his offer . . . until they got wind of the foul stink. 'Jesus, fella!' one of them exclaimed disgustedly. 'You must have been swimming in something mighty bad.'

Belching loudly, Baxter drew nearer to one of the flaming torches and peered myopically at them in the flickering light. 'Aw, don't take on so. It ain't like it's puke or such.'

His reluctant audience never got the chance to comment on that as the sound of pounding boots suddenly reached them; there was a sudden rush of movement as the 'drunk's' cronies erupted from the gloom. In the vicious mêlée that broke out, Baxter was knocked full length by his own boss; the precious bottle of 'joy juice' shattering on the side of the keel-boat.

Teach seized hold of one luckless guard and head-butted him full in the face, before finishing him off with a ferociously lethal chop to the throat. Another groaned in acute agony, as a Bowie knife was abruptly buried up to its hilt in his soft belly and then cruelly twisted before being withdrawn. Only one of the doomed sentinels got the chance to fight back. Momentarily separated from his assailants by Baxter's prone figure, the lone survivor drew and cocked his Schofield revolver. Yet before he could fire, Naylor swung his ancient Spencer carbine in a great roundhouse sweep, so that the stock smashed into the guard's unprotected skull. Perversely, it was the shock of that brutal blow that caused the man's right forefinger to contract.

The sudden detonation, in the stillness of the night, sounded like a cannon discharging. Teach, always on a hair trigger, was almost beside himself with rage. 'You stupid bastards. I said no shooting!'

The fourth member of the gang, a swarthy knife-fighter by the name of Rio, had the sense enough to realize that this was no time for recriminations. Gripping his blood-soaked Bowie he opined, 'It weren't nobody's fault and what's done is done. We need to get the hell out of here.'

'I give the orders,' Teach retorted belligerently, but then a cry of alarm in the darkened camp abruptly concentrated his mind. 'We needs to go. Get on the damn boat and find the poles. Rio, use your toad-stabber to cut through the ropes.'

That man hesitated. 'We might need them for tying up down stream, boss.'

More loud voices sounded from behind them. The alarm had well and truly been raised and Teach's patience was exhausted. 'We don't get moving, there won't be any down stream. Just cut the poxy cables!'

As his men clambered onto the cigar-shaped, shallow-drafted craft, the big, unkempt brute had an inspiration. Rushing to the nearest pitch torch, Teach grabbed it and thrust it into a gap in the landing stage planking. Even as he joined his cronies on board, the flames began to spread. He gave no thought to their three victims, even though one of them was quite possibly still alive.

'After this they'll maybe treat us better next time,' he snarled with decidedly perverse reasoning, although his next remark demonstrated that he did possess at least half a brain. Noticing that the knife-fighter was making for the rear cable, Teach bawled out, 'Not that one, shit for brains. Get the front one first, or the current'll swing us around.'

The other man stared at him dumbly for a moment before comprehending. Then, without a word, Rio raced the full length of the boat. Anger at the slight burned deep within him and fuelled his actions, because, in truth, it was very rare that he made a mistake. He furiously sliced through the forward cable, Teach took up a thick pole and placed the far end against the side of the burning jetty.

10

'Come on, come on,' the big man urged.

Finally there was a shout of triumph and the front of the boat began to ease away from the jetty. It couldn't come soon enough for the increasingly nervous thieves. Fresh torches had flared up in the camp and were now moving rapidly towards the river. As Rio scurried back towards the rear, Teach bellowed, 'Move yourself. They're nearly on us.'

As if to emphasize the dire urgency, a warning shot rang out, followed by a booming voice. 'Get off that boat, you sons of bitches!'

As the swarthy desperado slashed at the thick rope, the approaching posse spotted the three bodies on the blazing landing stage and a collective howl of anger went up. More shots exploded; the muzzle flashes briefly flaring in the night and this time hot lead slammed into the keelboat's timbers. What had initially seemed like a good plan appeared to be going disastrously wrong.

Then Naylor opened up with his battered Spencer. It was an old gun, but a repeater nonetheless. The return fire gave the angry miners pause and at that moment Rio uttered another exultant cry as the severed cable dropped into the water. With the keelboat no longer restrained and Teach manically heaving on his pole, the blazing jetty abruptly fell away.

Taken up by the current, the craft rapidly picked up speed and anger turned to frustration on the riverbank. Another ragged volley of shots boomed out. Apparently oblivious to the bullets smacking

11

home all around him, Rio – fired up by the exertion and excitement – mockingly waved at the rapidly receding camp. Gleefully, he yelled out, '*Huzzah*, you limp-dicked sons of bitches.' Then to his companions he added, 'We done showed those cockchafers a thing or two.'

In a matter of moments, the sleek craft had been swallowed up by the gloom and all that could be seen of Canon City was the inferno that had been a landing stage. It was then that all high spirits abruptly left the outlaws, as they were confronted by the reality of their new life on the river. A strained silence settled over them for some time, as all four men struggled to gain control over the boat using the long poles that they had found. The long, heavily laden craft seemed to possess a life of its own as it veered alarmingly from side to side.

Then Teach noticed the ten-foot long steering oar attached to a swivel at the rear and suddenly everything became so simple. With the barely visible riverbanks sliding by on either side and the Arkansas doing all the work, the novice pirates were suddenly able to relax.

Teach uttered a great sigh of relief. 'Hot dang. We made it. We'll put a few more miles between us and that camp and then pull into the far bank for the rest of the night.' He glanced over at Baxter and was surprised to see glum, downcast features. 'What the hell ails you, Barf?' he snapped. 'We've actually done good for a change!'

The foul-smelling outlaw stared at him sullenly. 'I

had my heart set on the rest of that bottle,' he mumbled, before adding accusingly, 'And *you* broke it!'

CHAPTER TWO

'This place got a name?'

Jacob Stuckey twitched with surprise and peered up from his task. With the Arkansas River flowing vigorously behind him, he had been so engrossed in daubing hot tar on the thick rope that he hadn't even heard the two horsemen arrive. And with only one hand, he most times had to concentrate that bit harder than most people. As they sat their saddles awaiting a response, he urged his slow mind into action.

'Not that I know of, mister. It just is, that's all.'

The bearded man tipped a battered, sweat-stained hat back on his head and sneered. '*Is* what?'

Jacob was confused. He sensed that the unexpected conversation was already going badly, but for the life of him he couldn't think why. Nervously, he tried again. 'It exists, just like it's always done, I guess.'

The second stranger, scrawny with a thin moustache, shook his head in disbelief. Like his companion, he was casually chewing tobacco. As he spoke, black juice seeped unpleasantly from the corners of his mouth. 'What kind of answer's that? It's got to have a name. Some kind of name. Otherwise how will we know where we've been?'

Jacob glanced over at the substantial log cabin, hoping that he might see John's burly figure, but the threshold remained unhelpfully empty. There was something about these two men that he didn't like and he vaguely recalled that in an earlier time he would have told them where to stick their curiosity . . . but he had been a different man then. In fact the whole country had been different. As it was, he didn't know what to say and so remained silent.

The bearded horseman felt no such constraints. 'Where'd you lose the arm, friend?'

Jacob placed the brush back in the tar pot and stood up. He could feel a flush coming to his features, as he always did at the mention of his disability. His right hand instinctively touched the empty sleeve and he suddenly recalled everything as though it was only the day before. Reluctantly, he replied, but in doing so supplied a little too much information. 'I was in Armistead's Brigade at Gettysburg. There was a fearful amount of violence in those three terrible days. I guess I was lucky to come out alive.'

The two men glanced darkly at each other, before the scrawny one venomously remarked, 'Fought under the Stars and Bars, eh. That'd make you a Johnny Reb, boy. And you know what? I lost my brother in that battle because he wasn't as *lucky* as you. He was a true Union man through and through, until some God damn rebel blew his head off!'

Jacob's flesh began to crawl as he gazed up at the hostile strangers. What was happening here? Only five minutes earlier, he hadn't possessed a care in the world. Yet now he was suddenly facing two trouble-makers all on his lonesome. And he suddenly noticed that they were leading two heavily laden pack mules. That most likely meant that they were out-lawed up and trading with the Indians. Feeling the adrenalin surge through his body, he desperately tried to keep his voice steady. 'It was all a long time ago, mister. Best just to let things lie.'

The lips under the thin moustache peeled back to display a set of gritted and discoloured teeth. 'Don't sass me, boy,' he snarled, as more tobacco juice leaked through them. 'You need to learn that some-times there just ain't no forgetting!' Even as he spoke, the scrawny individual's right hand drifted towards the Colt Army strapped to his waist.

With his guts beginning to churn, bile rose in Jacob's throat. It was thirteen years since anyone had shot at him, but the terror was suddenly immediate. 'Please, mister,' he pleaded. 'If I said something to upset you, it weren't meant and I'm real sorry.'

The two men merely stared fixedly at him as though he was just some kind of insect to be crushed.

'*Are you fellas always this much fun?*' The strong voice emanated from the cabin's entrance and sud-denly everything had changed. As Jacob breathed a sigh of relief, the hand of his tormentor froze just short of the revolver butt. Then, very slowly, the two men urged their animals to the left, so as to scrutinize the speaker. What they saw gave them pause for thought.

To their jaundiced eyes he appeared to be built like a house side. Exceptionally tall and broad, with jet-black hair, he was leaning casually against the building's inner doorframe. Worryingly, his hands were out of sight above the top rail and so could easily have been holding a weapon. Since neither of the startled horsemen appeared to be in any all-fired hurry to answer him, the occupant of the cabin carried on in an even, but strangely menacing tone.

'My name's Taggart. John Taggart. I own this cabin, the outbuildings and the ferry waiting over yonder. Since that's very probably what brings you here, I'd advise you not to provoke me.'

The two men regarded him warily. Hideout weapons were always unpredictable. The bearded one forced a smile. 'Hell, we ain't looking for trouble, friend. Just thought to bring you some ferrying business, is all.'

Taggart returned the smile, but it completely failed to reach his eyes. 'The crossing'll cost you one shiny silver dollar apiece. The horses and mules go free, on account of they don't cuss and cause trouble like human folks.'

The other man's apparent good cheer fled as he digested the cost. 'Sweet Jesus! Two dollars! That's daylight robbery. Most other crossing's are twenty cents.'

Taggart nodded. 'Aha. You're right on both counts. But since anyone wanting to cross over into the Indian Territories is likely to be on the run from something, I reckon it's a price worth paying. Especially as this is the *only* ferry along this stretch of water.'

The two strangers more or less simultaneously spat out their plugs of tobacco and then stared hard at each other. Whatever passed between them served its purpose, because they nodded almost imperceptibly.

'Good for you,' Taggart remarked brightly. 'Now you hand your coin over to Jacob. He's the fella with only one arm you were visiting with. Then just mosey on over to the ferry. I'll be there in a moment.' With that, he swiftly backed off into the gloom of the interior.

The two *fugitives*, because that was surely what they were, glowered at the abruptly empty threshold and then grudgingly handed over their money.

'You and I aren't through yet,' muttered the scrawny one darkly, before urging his horse over to the timber landing stage.

Keeping his distance from them, Jacob hurried over to remove the single pole that barred entry to the ferry. Although missing a limb, he tucked the barrier in the crook of his arm and effortlessly slid it to one side. The craft was well weathered, but strongly constructed and for the past six years had been easily capable of transporting even the heavily laden wagons that occasionally made the crossing. It had been painstakingly assembled during the summer of 1870, using two layers of fashioned tree trunks roped together at right angles. The deck planking had been brought by wagon all the way from a sawmill in Wichita, a good day's ride to the north. More rough-cut timber had then been used to build two solid sidewalls.

A single massive rope cable stretched from bank to bank. It was fed through a series of iron pulleys, which kept it firmly anchored to one side of the ferry, whilst at the same time allowed the operators to haul on it. On the northern, Kansas side, the cable was secured to a large beech tree, whilst to the south a huge boulder had been utilized. Once across, most people considered themselves to be in the Cherokee Nation and beyond the law's reach, but in fact were actually still in the United States proper.

Staying well away from the now dismounted passengers as they led their four animals aboard, Jacob removed a single leather glove from his pocket and using his teeth, deftly slipped it over his hand. As though assessing their future, the two men gazed keenly over at the far bank and so failed to observe the powerful figure of John Taggart, as he emerged from the cabin and strode over to the waiting ferry. Under one arm he carried a short blanket roll that seemed incongruous on such a warm summer's day. As his heavy footsteps sounded on the planking, his customers turned and glanced curiously at the bundle as he placed it on the deck.

'Day like this, I owe it to myself to stretch out under the sun over there,' he remarked casually and then nodded at his companion. With practised ease, the two men soon had the craft scudding across the fast flowing river. It was obvious to anyone who cared to watch that John was doing most of the work. His powerful shoulders bulged under the light cotton shirt and even with the gentle breeze beads of sweat soon formed on his face.

In spite of himself, the bearded man couldn't help but be impressed. 'Seems like you could handle this all on your lonesome,' he remarked with a scornful glance over at Jacob.

John glanced at him with eyes that were like chips of ice, before abruptly letting go of the cable and stalking over to his rolled blanket. With progress noticeably slowing, the two passengers watched with surprise, but no apparent alarm, as he reached down to retrieve something from the folds of material. Nothing could have prepared them for the sudden appearance of a cut down twelve-gauge shotgun, as John retracted both hammers and pointed the gaping muzzles directly at them. Even the stock had been removed; leaving just a stubby grip that seemed somehow to emphasize the weapon's lethal nature.

'The cartridges in this crowd pleaser are my own loads,' he conversationally announced. 'They're full of rusting off cuts from back when we built the cabin. If they don't kill you straight away, they'll sure as hell infect the wound.'

It was the scrawny individual who recovered first. 'Sweet Jesus, mister. We done paid the fare. *Ask him.* He'll tell you.'

'This ain't about money, you son of a bitch. I'm no road agent. Jacob is my friend. He saved my life in that same war you were jawing about. You treated him like shit and now you're going to pay.'

The other man's eyes widened like saucers. 'For Christ's sake, we didn't mean anything by it. We were just funning, is all.'

'Well he didn't look amused to me.' John's voice momentarily softened. 'Were you, Jacob?'

His friend appeared dumbstruck at the turn of events and merely shook his head silently.

John's eyes bored into his two prisoners. 'And if you slack jawed faggots had had any schooling, you'd know that the Mason–Dixon Line is a good piece to the north and east of here, which means that most anybody living around these parts are likely to have supported the Confederacy. So what you're going to do,' the big man continued remorselessly, 'Is unbuckle those gun belts and then toss them and all your shooting irons overboard. That way you won't be threatening any more innocent folks for a while.'

The two seedy looking outlaws were horrified. 'You can't send us down into the Territories without any firearms. We've got business to attend to with some real touchy folks. We'll end up dead as a wagon tyre.'

John's grim expression offered them not so much as a crumb of comfort. 'Maybe you will and maybe you won't, but you should have thought about that before picking on my friend. Now do it or get to dying!'

21

The men's features registered bitter loathing, but they knew better than to argue with a levelled sawn-off. Slowly and very reluctantly they pitched their weapons into the Arkansas River. First went the holster guns and then the rifles. Their weight ensured that they would sink straight to the bottom.

'You can keep your knives for whittling and such,' John remarked, 'But I'll be having the hide-outs.'

Their expressions darkened even more, as the contents of two shoulder holsters were surrendered to the water. Only then did their persecutor nod to Jacob. 'You can ease us into the bank now and then these gentlemen can be on their way. I reckon this is one ride they won't forget in a hurry.'

Moments later, the two men were leading their horses and mules off the ferry. Once mounted and on the move, their courage rapidly returned. 'You'll pay for this in spades, you bastards,' snarled the smaller of the two. 'Just see if you don't. We'll be back here one day, when you least expect it.'

John carefully lowered the hammers on his shotgun. 'I'll look forward to it,' he hollered back. 'We're always open for business. And just so as you know, this place is called Taggart's Crossing.'

'I never knew that,' Jacob innocently remarked, no longer tongue tied now that the outlaws had departed.

'Well then, it just goes to show that you learn something everyday,' John replied with a broad smile. 'And what those fellows learned is that nobody messes with John Taggart.'

CHAPTER THREE

'How do you know they'll chase us?'

Russ Decker sighed impatiently. A big, bluff individual, he possessed a sharp mind and did not suffer fools gladly. He well knew that not all the members of his gang were playing with a full deck, but he endured their presence because someone had to make up the numbers.

'Because this town's booming,' he quickly responded. 'Just like any cowtown situated on a railhead. It's awash with money. Which means the banks have lots of cash in them and the good citizens ain't going to like us taking it. That's why I've got a plan for afterwards.'

'Aren't you going to tell us?' whined the third man.

'No, Brett. I ain't,' Decker responded emphatically. 'Because if I told you everything up front, you'd get to thinking you didn't need me anymore. But you'd be sorely wrong!'

The three horsemen had just crossed over the

tracks of the Atchison, Topeka and Santa Fe Railroad, at the point where the well used rails swept into the northern end of town. Stockyards full of lowing beasts dominated the area, reinforcing that fact that this was definitely cattle country. Wichita, Kansas was the county seat of Sedgwick County and a substantial settlement. It possessed a fine red brick courthouse, a United States Land Office and various newspaper offices. The buildings had an air of permanence about them, with a good many being built from brick and native limestone. All of this hinted at affluence and such circumstances would always attract undesirables. Which, of course, was exactly what the newcomers were.

The men deliberately maintained an unhurried pace, as they made their way onto the start of Santa Fe Street. They all wore duster coats, which had once been white but were now yellowed by age and usage. The warm dry weather ensured that they were uncomfortable, but the coats concealed an unusual amount of weaponry carried by supposedly innocent visitors. Split up the back to hip level for use on horseback, they also enabled the wearer to draw a holstered weapon with ease.

As they plodded along, Decker suddenly favoured an ancient citizen with a beaming smile. The old man was passing time on a porch stoop and had no inkling that the affable greeting was actually a display of relief. The lead horseman had just spotted three more men wearing identical garb, who had just come into view at the far end of the long thoroughfare. In his heart, he had known that Lansing wouldn't mess up, but there was always a first time for everything.

'Remember,' he ordered softly. 'You two hitch your animals opposite the bank and make out you're having trouble with a cinch or something. No shooting unless someone else starts it. I want dollars, not deaths!'

His two companions grunted. They were going on a bank robbery, not a church social. If anyone got in their way, there would have to be some blood spilt and from past experience, their boss was more than willing to take a life.

Down the street, Mark Lansing had just given similar instructions to his men, but he was pragmatic enough to recognize that in the heat of the moment things could simply just happen. Lean and angular, with sideburns and a luxuriant moustache, he was in effect Decker's right-hand-man and no stranger to bloody violence. But that didn't mean he took any pleasure in it. In fact, of late, his enthusiasm for life on the dodge had waned considerably. The years of hard living were weighing heavily on him and he was feeling distinctly world-weary.

The two groups finally reined in at staggered intervals opposite the Farmers' and Merchants' Bank; two men directly outside and four at the far side of the wide dirt street. The bank's premises were in an imposing two-storey structure built of red brick. To the eager eyes of the new arrivals it held a great deal of promise.

Decker and Lansing nodded genially at each

other, as though they were associates meeting to conduct business. Next they glanced seemingly casually around, checking rooftops and shop fronts for any sign of ambush. Wichita's citizens appeared to be going about their daily lives without any apparent concern, but Decker was keen to get off the street. He was well aware that sooner or later, six men in identical duster coats would attract attention.

'Let's get this done,' he remarked and headed for the entrance. His left hand, inserted into a non-existent coat pocket, clutched the fore stock of a sawn-off shotgun.

The two men, spurs clinking noisily, strode across the timbered sidewalk and through the open double doors. Conveniently, there was only one other customer in the place. Wearing an apron and exchanging notes for coins, he was obviously a storekeeper of some kind.

The interior was spacious and inviting. Varnished floorboards gleamed like the highly polished counter, which effectively split the ground floor into two halves. The counter was roughly waist-high, but above it a wire mesh structure reached up another three feet. This made for some imposing height, but had little chance of stopping a bullet. An access door, for those clients who warranted greater attention, was situated to the side of the teller positions. Beyond those lay various desks manned by men in store-bought suits. Up against the back wall stood the largest iron safe that either of them had ever seen. With only one visible armed guard, it was going to be like taking candy from a baby.

That individual, large and capable looking, was leaning against the right hand wall with a Winchester cradled in the crook of his left arm. As the two travel-stained customers clanked into the room, he scrutinized them carefully. They were obviously from out of town and that in itself made them worth a second look. Unfortunately for the bank employee, he was just one man unknowingly confronted by a pair of hardened professionals.

Decker nodded to his accomplice and then made directly for the nearest teller. Lansing veered off to the right, ostensibly to fill out a deposit slip on one of the tables near the guard. Decker's right hand slipped inside his open coat and that action was enough to abruptly claim all the sentinel's attention. Instinctively pulling clear of the wall, that man unwittingly left himself open and the other bank robber took full advantage.

Lansing's hand deftly slipped through the rear slit of his duster, seized the Remington around its cylinder and with a sweeping motion brought the butt crashing down onto an unprotected skull. With a shuddering sigh, the luckless guard toppled to the floor and lay still. Even as he did so, Decker drew his own revolver and pointed it directly at the startled face of the nearest teller. He kept his voice low, but it positively dripped menace.

'Unless you want your brains all over this shiny counter, keep your hands in sight and open the God damn door!'

27

Simultaneously, Lansing cocked and pointed his weapon at the storekeeper and barked out, 'Get on the floor and sit on your hands, now!'

Eyes wide with shock, the man did exactly that and the bank employee hesitated for only a moment before following Decker's instructions. As the bolt slid back, the outlaw stepped onto the bank's hallowed ground and gazed around at the horrified staff. There appeared to be some kind of manager clad in a sharp suit and three tellers, all apparently unarmed.

'Let's make this easy,' the gunman growled. 'I only want the bank's money, not yours. So none of this is worth dying for.' He glanced round as two of his gang entered the premises carrying canvas bags. 'Empty the cash drawers first,' he barked out. 'Paper money only.'

As the men complied, he holstered his revolver and replaced it with the sawn-off shotgun from under his coat. The portly manager's eyes boggled, as the gaping muzzles swung over to cover him. 'Please don't hurt me!' he gasped out.

Decker favoured him with a cold smile. 'Just open the safe,' he commanded.

The other man visibly trembled with fear and words came in a flood. 'I can't. I haven't got a key. Only the president, Mister A.W. Clark has one and he's out of town. We've been robbed before, so we normally only keep enough cash in the drawers for the one day. Because he's away for a few days, there's a lot more than usual under the counter, so you're in luck. Please, mister. Don't shoot. It's the God's honest truth. I wasn't raised to lie!'

Decker stared at him long and hard. He came to a decision just as one of his men snarled, 'The son of a bitch is lying, boss. Blow one of his fingers off. That'll get the safe open quick enough.'

The outlaw leader shook his head dismissively. 'Nah, I reckon he's telling the truth. You ought to try it sometime.'

That short exchange resulted in an unexpected bonus. The manager's relief was plain to see. Completely overcome, he uttered a massive sigh and without warning his legs gave way. As he collapsed to the floor, the poor man pointed at a dull green strongbox half hidden under the counter. 'I haven't got the key for that either, but just take it and go!'

Decker's eyes lit up with pure avarice. He recognised a Wells Fargo cashbox when he saw one. The ubiquitous freight company used them to transfer valuables from town to town by stagecoach. The padlock on this one was massive. It would require a blacksmith's tools to remove it. Moving fast, he seized the box with one hand. He grunted with the effort required to lift it and then smiled broadly. There was an awful lot of something inside. His men had cleared the drawers. It was time to leave. 'Let's get the hell out of here,' he barked. With that, the three of them swept through the door in the counter and it was about then that everything started to unravel.

Lansing glanced dubiously at the strongbox. He too knew whom it belonged to. 'For God's sake, Russ.

That thing'll be more trouble than a sack full of rat-tlesnakes. Dump it and let's go!'

Decker shook his head stubbornly. 'I believe in money, not God. You know that. Besides, this thing is heavy. Real heavy! Which means our luck has changed and since our bullets won't break that shackle, it's coming with us.'

At that moment, a customer with cash to deposit appeared in the doorway. He was a hard-bitten ex-army type, who immediately recognized trouble and thought he could handle it. No 'saddle tramps' were going to take his money. By reaching for the gun at his waist, he left the outlaws no option.

Josh, the gang member who had been so keen to spill some blood, fired first, followed swiftly by Mark Lansing. With two bullets lodged in his chest, the new arrival staggered back onto the boardwalk and reflexively discharged his revolver into the timber. He was dead before he hit the ground and lay there wreathed in smoke, blood soaking into his jacket. With one man slain, the outlaws recognized that it no longer mattered how many more died in Wichita. Their own survival was now the only concern.

The sudden outbreak of bloody violence galva-nized all six bank robbers into action. The two on the far side of the street quickly mounted up and drew their weapons. They knew that the best way to get out of town alive was to intimidate the citizens by a show of force. Accordingly, they urged their horses into motion and began shooting at windows and into the air. Screams joined the deafening crash of firearms and shattering glass, as the townsfolk desperately rushed to get off the street without being either shot or trampled.

Town Marshal Todd Turner's substantial frame was comfortably settled in his usual chair at the barber's. He was a man whose responsibilities of office weighed lightly upon him. A creature of habit, he always arrived for his morning shave at the same time. The white lather had just nicely coated his stubble when the first shots rang out.

'Aw hell,' he complained. 'Why did someone have to go and do that?'

Then the firing started in earnest and he was out of his chair and heading for the door. The lawman yanked it open just as one of the duster clad riders galloped past. A heavy bullet smashed into the door-frame next to his head, sending a wicked splinter slicing into his left cheek. Howling with pain, he leapt back into the shop and slammed the door shut. His revolver had not even left its holster and he was already out of the fight. Locking up drunken trail-hands at one dollar each arrest was one thing, but a deadly shooting match entirely another.

As Santa Fe Street cleared of traffic, Decker yelled at his friend and sidekick. 'Help me rope this damn thing to the saddle.'

The horses, stirred up by the shooting, were tugging against their tethered reins. The two mounted outlaws were careering about the dirt street, screaming abuse and firing indiscriminately. And yet, in spite of the urgency, Lansing held off.

'No good will come of taking it.' He gestured behind him. 'That's just one bank amongst many, but this box represents so much more. Take my advice and leave it, or we'll have all kinds of law after us!'

Decker again shook his head obstinately. 'Let them come. It's a big country. Don't you understand? We did good in there, but with this we'll do better.'

Across the street, a shot rang out and this time it wasn't from one of his men. The town was starting to fight back. Another gun fired and a piece of the hitching rail disintegrated. Someone had got up onto a rooftop.

Decker began to get well and truly angry. 'For Christ's sake, Mark, are you with me or agin me?'

Lansing stared hard at him for a moment. Then one of their men cried out, 'Shit in a bucket, fellas. We've stirred up a hornet's nest. Let's move ass,' and against his better judgment he grabbed the coil of rope from his saddle and helped his boss to secure the strongbox. It would very likely slow them down, but the die was cast and there was no going back. Just at that moment, as though emphasizing the fact, a vastly more potent rifle opened up.

The bank robbers could not possibly have foreseen it, but there was another lawman in Wichita that day and he had far more on his mind than just a close shave. Deputy United States Marshal Sam Torrance had a wanted man locked up in the town jail. He was intending to leave very shortly to deliver him to Judge Parker's Federal Court in Fort Smith. When the first shot rang out, the seasoned enforcer was draining his second cup of coffee in McCready's Eating House. Well accustomed to the harsher aspects of upholding the law, he reached for the Winchester Model 1876 rifle that he habitually carried and strode to the door.

Pounding hoofs and rapid gunfire supplied broad hints as to just what was afoot and the marshal was not a man to take unnecessary risks. Dropping onto his haunches, he levered up a powerful .45-.75 cartridge and carefully eased open the door. Out on the street there was mayhem, with men, women and children desperately running for cover to escape two rampaging gunmen in grubby duster coats. Four more of them were clustered over by the bank, apparently resolving some heated dispute. To the marshal's logical mind, it seemed a hell of a place for an argument, but then there was just no accounting for some folk's behaviour. Although sporadic shots rang out from the surrounding buildings, it was obvious that the town needed professional help.

Instinctively aiming for a large target, Torrance rapidly drew a bead on the nearest marauder's horse and fired. No one with his experience could have missed at such range and sure enough the unfortunate creature slewed sideways and crashed to the ground. Its rider, a vicious individual named Huey Soble, just managed to throw himself clear and athletically turned a bad fall into a controlled roll. Getting to his feet with surprising ease, the outlaw found that entirely by chance he was facing the eating house rather than his comrades. The lawman smiled grimly at what had surely been a waste of effort on his victim's part and smoothly worked the lever action. Again he took aim, but this time at human prey.

Even as his man 'bit the dust' to the sound of a much deeper discharge, Russ Decker recognized that the situation had abruptly changed. In that brief moment he saw it all. Only two kinds of men used such a powerful weapon, either buffalo hunters or man hunters. Odds on, they now had a proficient 'law dog' to contend with. Rapidly scanning the surrounding buildings, he spotted a rifle barrel poking through the threshold of McCready's diagonally down the street. Quickly levelling his own shotgun, the outlaw leader squeezed both triggers a mere split-second before their opponent fired.

With a sawn-off only really deadly at close range, the contents of the two twelve gauge cartridges acted as more of a deterrent. As the barrage of pellets spattered the front of the eating-house, only one actually struck Marshal Torrance, but that was enough to affect his aim. The small piece of lead tore through the left sleeve of his linen shirt, creating a minor flesh wound in his upper arm. The shock was enough to jerk the Winchester's barrel to the right at the very instant that he fired.

Soble, disorientated from the fall, had only just got to his feet when the bullet smashed into his left shoulder and sent him reeling backwards into the dust. This time it took him far longer to get up and when he did fresh blood stained his long coat.

All the other men were now mounted and Decker bellowed at the one with the strongest animal. 'Nobody gets left behind. Huey can ride double with you until we steal another horse.'

As the powerfully mounted man raced off to comply, his cronies fired at anything that moved. The citizen on the roof showed himself once too often and Lansing shot him dead centre, bringing the unfortunate tumbling down to the sidewalk with bone-breaking force. Then all the raiders, including Soble, were in the saddle and without any further hindrance they galloped off, heading south. At Decker's insistence, they made one brief stop at the blacksmith's forge just inside the town's limits, to relieve the angry tradesman of a large hammer. Then they were off again, six fugitives with blood on their hands.

An eerie silence fell on Santa Fe Street, disturbed only by the pitiful whinnying of the mortally-wounded horse. As the small clouds of gun smoke gradually dispersed, so the people of Wichita cautiously reappeared. Sam Torrance hated unnecessary suffering and so resolutely approached the stricken beast. Carefully aiming his rifle at its head, he squeezed the trigger. As the loud report crashed out, there was momentary alarm that brought a cynical smile to the lawman's weathered face.

The Decker gang's raid on the Farmers' and Merchants' Bank had resulted in the deaths of at least two men and a great deal of broken glass. There had been robberies before, but this one had been bloodier than most. Another feature set this robbery apart – the Wells Fargo box; this contained US Mail, which meant that federal law had been broken. Like it or not, Marshal Torrance now had another duty to perform.

CHAPTER FOUR

'So what are your intentions?'

Sam Torrance favoured Turner with a sidelong glance. He was not about to discuss his plans with some lily-livered town marshal. For all he knew the man might actually have been in on the raid and was now trading on the flesh wound to look good in front of the townspeople. Consequently he merely pointed dismissively towards the prisoner languishing in one of the jail's three cells.

'I'm charged with delivering that sack of shit to Fort Smith, so that's what I'm going to do. If I should happen to trip over a gang of bank robbers on the way, then I'll arrest them, but it seems unlikely. They'll be hotfooting it south to the Indian Territories, whereas I'm heading east.'

There was a grating whine from the sour-looking character behind bars. 'Aw, you shouldn't ought to talk about me like that, marshal. I've got feelings too.'

Torrance looked scathingly over at him. 'Yeah and so had those young girls you kidnapped and sold on, you piss-streaked pile of puke!'

Marshal Turner's eyes widened at the sharp exchange. He would be damn glad to get *both* men off his premises. He was used to a quiet life and the presence of the federal officer uncomfortably reminded him of just how the law was *supposed* to be enforced.

'So you'll likely be leaving us soon,' he remarked hopefully.

The US Marshal chuckled mirthlessly. 'Right this very minute, actually. That way you'll be able to get on with raising a posse of your own, without my interference.' As Wichita's lawman coloured with embarrassment, he added, 'And if that *wound* should happen to slow you down, I wouldn't worry overmuch. After what's happened here, you can bet your bottom dollar that the Pinkertons will be swarming all over this place mighty soon.'

It wasn't until later that afternoon that Jonas Bills realized he had been listening to a load of hogwash. 'Hey, we ain't travelling east at all. You was just joshing with that Wichita law-dog.'

Marshal Torrance reluctantly switched his gaze from the terrain ahead and regarded his diminutive prisoner disdainfully. The man was riding along next to him, his right hand manacled to the saddle horn. 'You're a pretty smart cuss for a felon. Working all that out on your lonesome.'

Bills possessed brutalized features and mean eyes

which were currently fixed on those of his captor. Completely missing the sarcasm, he continued airing his train of thought. 'Which means you're really going after that gang. And if they put up a fight, I'm just as likely to catch a bullet as you, which sure ain't my idea of justice!'

Torrance scoffed at his captive's concern. 'You should have thought of that before doing your bad deeds. As for me, I don't aim to stumble in too close. One of them has already given me a flesh wound with his God damned sawn-off.' Patting the stock of his Winchester, he continued, 'This fine rifle can soften them up a bit first. Make them see the error of their ways. I reckon I know where they're headed and a day's ride should prove me right . . . or wrong. Either way, where I go, you go and that's just the way it is.'

Bills' eyes narrowed as he digested that. 'And where might that be?'

The lawman pondered a moment, before deciding that there could be no harm in disclosing their immediate destination. 'A ferry crossing on the Arkansas River. If those sons of bitches are heading for the Indian Territories, which I believe they are, then they have to use it. It's the only one for miles around. Now shut your mouth. I'm done talking!'

Bills muttered something unintelligible before sinking into, what was for him, deep thought. It occurred to him, as they made their way southwards across the rolling grasslands of the Great Plains that this unexpected detour might just pan out to his advantage. The marshal's pre-occupation with bank robbers could be that lawman's undoing – Jonas Bills wasn't someone you turned your back on. One thing was for sure; the kidnapper *and* murderer had no intention whatsoever of dangling from Judge Parker's noose!

'Where the hell are you taking us, boss?' Huey Soble demanded bitterly. He was hurting bad and in no mood for lengthy excursions. 'If we carry on like this, we'll be in God damned Missouri afore long!'

Russ Decker glanced darkly over at his minion, but decided to make allowances. Although the wounded man was swaying theatrically in his saddle, he was undoubtedly in a lot of pain. In spite of the makeshift bandage, his shirt was soaked with blood and the man riding double with him was in no itching hurry to hold him close.

'Just you hush now, Huey,' he said softly. 'What with being a horse short and toting this box, we can't outrun whoever's after us. So I've taken us off to the east a ways. Any posse will expect us to head straight for the river crossing and then hide up in the Indian Nations. Which means they'll end up chasing a non-existent trail until they get bored and go home.'

The six men had ridden up into the hill country to the south east of Wichita, where the plains finally petered out. It was rough ground. Any pursuers would be unlikely to follow them without the help of an Indian tracker. And yet they couldn't stay there forever. The only relatively safe haven was in the Indian Territories, where there were no white settlements.

Mark Lansing glanced over at a small grove of trees. 'I reckon that'll serve, Russ. Nobody will see us at a distance in there. We can get the bullet out of his shoulder and open up that damn box. Whatever's in there will be a lot easier to carry, if it's spread across the six of us . . . Don't you think?' He knew from old that it was better to offer his boss the illusion that he had come up with any idea.

Decker considered the natural canopy. The shade did look inviting and he was undeniably curious as to the contents of the green Wells Fargo box. And Soble's groaning was getting on his nerves. 'We'll camp in those trees,' he announced decisively. 'Get a fire going. A small one mind and no leaves.' His eyes met those of his subordinate. 'You'd better be the one to get that ball out. Your hand is plenty steady *and* you've done it before.'

Lansing regarded him ruefully. 'Thanks, boss. You're all heart.'

With the horses tethered and an almost smokeless fire burning, Decker left his men to it. They all knew well enough the basics of campfire surgery and he was now consumed by greedy anticipation. Even as Soble was placed none too gently down next to the fire, the gang leader unfastened the rope binding around the strongbox and lowered it to the ground. It sure was a heavy son of a bitch!

Whilst Lansing cut away the blood-soaked shirt, his boss firmly grasped the stolen hammer. Soble had already consumed close on a pint of cheap whiskey, but as a leather knife scabbard was placed between his teeth, he still knew full well what was to come. As the knife point approached the throbbing and *very* tender wound, the terrified outlaw's eyes were wide with fear.

A massive blow struck the padlock and Lansing jerked with surprise. 'God damn it, Russ. I nearly took his ear off then.'

Decker affected little concern. 'Pretend you're a battlefield surgeon. They had to put up with all sorts of distractions.' With that, he unleashed another tremendous clout that brought sparks flying. His men were torn between their duty to a comrade and instinctive avarice.

'Hold him steady, damn you,' Lansing barked testily. With that, he eased his blade into the torn flesh and probed gingerly for the lead bullet. With sweat poring from his brow, Soble went rigid and moaned pitifully. The tendons stood out on his neck, as he bit into the tough leather. Another crash came from the strongbox, but this time the amateur sawbones was ready for it. With desperate concentration, he penetrated ever deeper into the bloody wound, until suddenly he came upon an obstruction that definitely wasn't bone.

'Found it,' Lansing announced to the accompaniment of yet another metallic crack.

'Shit in a bucket!' Decker exclaimed. 'Who forged this poxy thing? We should have taken the blacksmith as well as his hammer.'

Completely ignoring him, his deputy snapped at

the three onlookers. 'This is going to test Huey badly. One of you get on his legs. The other two on his arms. Quickly now.'

Once they'd complied, he angled the blade slightly and applied pressure against the flesh's suction. Soble's moans intensified and he struggled ever more violently. Then, with a great cry of satisfaction, Lansing held up the rifle bullet with his bloodied fingers for all to see, but he wasn't to keep his audience for long. At that very moment, Decker let rip with a tremendous blow and the shackle finally surrendered to his determined assault. With the padlock in pieces on the grass, he yanked open the lid and peered eagerly inside.

Lansing abruptly found himself alone with his suffering patient, but had one more unpleasant duty to perform. Surreptitiously, he pulled the cork out of Soble's whiskey bottle and took a quick swig. Then, without any warning, he poured the remains of the fiery liquid over the livid wound and leapt back out of range. Without anyone to restrain him, the anguished outlaw flailed around like a berserker. Even then, his pathetic antics merited only a casual glance from his cronies, because their attention was most definitely elsewhere.

Decker pawed eagerly through the contents of the strongbox. The wads of paper money were a positive, the packets of US Mail less so. He well knew that the theft of them might attract the unwelcome attention of federal marshals. Then he hefted an innocuous looking, thick canvas bag and his eyes lit up.

Whatever was in it had definitely contributed to the weight. Excitedly, he cut through the draw cord at the neck and upended the bag. Its dazzling contents spilled out into the box.

'Sweet Jesus,' he exclaimed. 'Will you look at that?'

Four pairs of feverish eyes stared at the pile of freshly minted, gleaming gold Double Eagles.

Ed Teach could feel his hackles rising yet again. Baxter's incessant whining and bellyaching was fast becoming intolerable. This was their third day on the narrow keelboat, surrounded by the seemingly limitless Great Plains and the enforced idleness was beginning to tell on them. Running at speed with the current, required that one man be permanently vigilant whilst steering the heavily laden craft, but the other three had absolutely nothing to occupy them. Doubts about Teach's 'grand plan' had begun to creep in, made worse by the fact that their volatile boss didn't have any answers to their questions and the novelty of being river pirates had long since worn off.

'All I'm saying,' Baxter droned on, 'Is I don't see how we're going to sell great lumps of silver ore in the Indian Territories. Who the hell's going to pay cash money for them?'

Such a depressing thought had already occurred to Teach, so his being reminded of it didn't help any. He had chosen to steer for a while, but was now regretting that decision. The necessity to grip the steering oar prevented him from seizing Baxter by the throat.

'Why didn't we steal it after it had been refined,' that man continued, seemingly oblivious to his leader's rising anger. 'Now that *would* have made sense, 'cause we could have forged coins or some such out of it. With proper cash money we could buy some real sipping whiskey, like they drink back east an' not the moose piss that we usually have to swig!'

Two completely unconnected things happened then. Up in the 'sharp' end, Naylor yelled back, 'There's a big town up ahead on the left bank, boss. Why not pull in and get some vittles?'

At the exact same moment, Ed Teach, always on a short fuse, abruptly lost all self-control. Oblivious to the approaching settlement, he recklessly cast the steering oar aside and surged down the outer wall of the enclosed cabin. His target was the suddenly speechless Baxter, who had been idly watching the grassland pass by as he rambled on. Out of control, the keelboat veered sharply towards the riverbank and threw the almost incandescent outlaw boss into the central structure with stunning force.

'Sweet Jesus!' Rio exclaimed. 'You'll kill us all.' So saying, he agilely raced around the other side of the cabin towards the stern. At the same time, Naylor hefted a pole in his hands, ready to make a vain attempt at fending off the rapidly approaching shore. If nothing else, his swift reaction proved that he had learned something on the voyage.

As Teach got his breath back, Baxter scurried away across the decking. He knew all too well what the huge, unkempt man was capable of and genuinely feared for his life. Realizing that he couldn't elude those huge paws forever, he even contemplated leaping into the Arkansas.

It was the ever-resourceful knife-fighter who saved the boat from certain destruction. Grabbing the steering pole, he heaved his end sharply over to the left and so ensured that the sharp angle came off their approach. Naylor gamely pushed against the solid timber jetty, but even so the keelboat smacked into it with a resounding thump. Following their rapid getaway from Canon City, they had discovered that only enough rope had been retained to tie up at the stern. As Rio leapt ashore to do just that, Baxter did the same up at the bow – except that Baxter's sole intention was to escape Teach's clutches.

It was only after the craft had been relatively safely moored that anyone took the trouble to really look around. And what they saw took their breath away. The grassland surrounding the settlement appeared to be covered by cows, or more precisely, Texas Longhorns. Trail hands were surging around the herd, or herds, directing the flow towards huge cattle pens and corrals. There could be no doubt that the silver thieves had arrived smack in the heart of cattle country.

A number of idlers and gawkers, some of them fishing off the jetty, regarded the new arrivals curiously. Four men seemed a very small crew for such a long vessel.

'Where the hell are we?' Teach muttered, still angry that Baxter had temporarily evaded his clutches.

One of the locals sniggered and pointed to a sign that had been haphazardly hammered into the ground next to the landing stage.

Welcome To Dodge City
No Firearms Allowed
Within The City Limits

'Hope you fellas like beef,' he remarked. 'It's pretty much all you'll get to eat around here. That and beans. We *never* seem run out of Goddamn beans!'

It was then that Baxter spotted a far more important feature of the frontier town. The main north-south thoroughfare was bisected by railroad tracks that came to an end just west of the settlement. 'We've fetched up slap bang next to a railhead,' he exulted, before adding far more quietly. 'All we need do is find a buyer. What say you, fellas?'

Teach stared at him, all enmity suddenly forgotten. 'What I say, Barf, is that it's past time that you visited a bathhouse. And if we do things right in this here Dodge City, you'll get that chance.'

It was Rio who displayed the least enthusiasm. 'I've never liked towns much, so I reckon I'll stay here and mind the store. There's only one rope holding this boat in place and in any case we can't just up and leave it without a guard.'

Teach had no problem with any of that. All his thoughts were now focused on possible opportunities in the cow town. 'That's hunky-dory with me. We'll be back before you know it with the cargo sold and our boots full of greenbacks. We might even bring you a drink!'

Rio stared at the departing trio and shook his head despairingly. Not for the first time he wondered just why he had ever joined up with them. After taking a good look around the mooring and its apparently harmless occupants, he settled down at the rear of the boat. Pretty soon the rocking motion combined with the warm sunshine to send him sound asleep.

The sun had long passed its zenith when the negligent sentry abruptly jerked awake. For a deliciously brief moment he had absolutely no idea where he was. Then a familiar bellow intruded and he was back to reality with a jolt. Rio's three cronies were frantically running towards the river, their extreme speed motivated by the need for self-preservation. Behind them, streaming out of Dodge City's bustling centre was an all too familiar angry mob.

'Oh, not again,' he sighed and clambered shakily to his feet.

'Cut the damn rope,' Teach hollered breathlessly. He tried to add something else, but his words were drowned out by gunfire as various citizens took wild shots at the fleeing men.

Realizing that they would never be able to tie up again, if he complied, Rio kept his Bowie sheathed and instead leapt onto the jetty. Working frenetically on the rope, he managed to prise it loose so that only

48

a loop around the post held the boat in place; once the others got aboard he would need to move fast.

The dirt thoroughfare known as Front Street was flanked to within a few yards of the mooring by timber buildings and so the three fugitives had had a gleeful and rowdy audience all the way. But the haphazard pursuit was about to turn deadly serious. A huge barrel of a man sporting a luxurious moustache and weighing in excess of three hundred pounds soon decided that running was both exhausting and unnecessary. As city marshal, he was well within his rights to use the revolver strapped to his ample girth.

Coming to a grinding halt, the 'man mountain' stood patiently for a few moments to get control of his ragged breathing. Then, drawing and cocking an immaculately maintained Remington, he very deliberately took aim at the largest of the fleeing men. As the lawman's weapon discharged with a satisfying crash, Ed Teach suddenly felt tearing agony in his left ear. It was as though a red-hot poker had been plunged into it and the shock nearly brought him to earth. With the keelboat now only feet away, he made a last ditch effort and surged towards it.

'Huh, must be pulling to the left a little,' grunted City Marshal Larry Deger as he again readied his weapon.

Finally, the outlaw boss reached the landing stage and threw himself bodily over the gunwale. His two cronies were close behind and the second that they were on board, Rio unfurled the rope and leapt into the stern. They weren't a moment too soon. Even as

49

he heaved on the steering oar, another well-aimed shot rang out and splinters flew off the boat's transom.

As the Arkansas' current carried the poleboat away from Dodge City, Teach angrily peered over the side. Blood poured from his mangled flesh and his savage mood wasn't improved by the sight of one of the inhabitants cupping a hand over his left ear.

'Don't look like you'll be *'earing* from Larry again,' a raucous voice yelled out, to the sound of much appreciative laughter on the riverbank. The hilarity followed the boat until they were finally out of sight.

'What the hell happened back there,' Rio enquired curiously. Even for men of their ilk, his companions had managed to stir up a veritable hornet's nest in a town where they were supposedly unknown. And it hadn't escaped his notice that Baxter had impressive bruising around his left eye.

It was some time before anyone replied. Teach was occupied with hanging over the side, scooping cool water up onto his throbbing wound. Baxter was casting increasingly nervous glances in his direction and as usual Naylor was content to let someone else do the talking. Only after their blood-soaked leader had flopped down onto the decking did Rio get some kind of answer.

'What the hell *didn't* happen?' came the sour response. Licking his lips, Teach favoured Baxter with a particularly malicious stare. 'We fetched up in a saloon called The Long Branch. It seemed like a good place to start. I bought a few drinks and got to talking with some fellas about our interesting cargo.'

Rio groaned inwardly. He could almost see the débâcle unfolding.

'Anyhow,' Teach continued. 'Barf here couldn't keep his eye on the mark. Took a fancy to a short whore name of Rowdy Kate. Afore long, she led him upstairs to tend to business. Only problem was, this knucklehead didn't have the special price she'd offered, but that didn't come out 'til afterwards. So what does he do? The silly bastard only goes and hits her!'

'She pulled a blade on me,' Baxter protested.

'Only after you'd tried to stove her head in,' Teach retorted. 'And she certainly lived up to her nickname, because then all hell broke loose. Turns out her regular customer just happened to be the city marshal. A huge son of a bitch, name of Deger. And you know what? He only comes after the two of us as well.'

Immediately comprehending the reason, Rio shook his head. 'Because you hadn't checked in your shooting irons.'

Teach glowered at him briefly, before returning his malevolent attention to Baxter. 'Before we knew it, that law-dog had deputized everyone in the room and we had to run for our lives. And I've lost half an ear, all because *you* couldn't keep it in your pants!'

Baxter regarded him warily. The keelboat was well away from either bank. There was no escape. 'It weren't my fault, boss,' he whined. 'I'd give *anything* for you not to have got hurt.'

'It might just come to that,' Teach remarked darkly, before abruptly looking away. 'Naylor, get over here and put some stitches in this, before I God damn bleed to death!'

That man sighed, but did as instructed and for the first time since their close escape actually offered an observation. 'And Barf never did make it to a bath-house. How that bitch could touch his pecker is beyond me!'

CHAPTER FIVE

'I want those bastards caught. Every last one of them, you hear?' Bank President A.W. Clark almost shouted the words.

It was the morning after the robbery in Wichita. He had arrived back from Kansas City at the urgent behest of his manager and to his jaundiced eyes, little seemed to have been done. The only plus point was the arrival of an employee of the Pinkerton Detective Agency. Ben Exley was his name and it was he who had been on the receiving end of the strident demand. A smooth-shaven city slicker in a store bought suit, he was well used to dealing with aggrieved clients.

'What about the city marshal?' he enquired. 'Did he deputize a posse?'

Clark snorted scornfully. He was a well-fed, florid individual, full of his own importance. He continued, 'That man Turner ain't worth moose piss. He got a little bitty splinter in his face and spent the rest of the day at the doctor's. You see that stain on the floor

there? That's where one of my customers was killed.'
Making a supreme effort, he managed to lower his
voice. 'And what really vexes me is the loss of a Wells
Fargo strongbox, full of Double Eagles. Because it was
on the bank's premises, we're liable and I'm not in
business to make a loss. So tell me, Mister Pinkerton
Agent, just what are you going to do about it?'

Exley was ambitious and highly regarded by Allan
Pinkerton. Regarding the bank president calmly,
Exley favoured him with a soothing smile. 'I've got
half a dozen of the agency's best men arriving by rail
this afternoon. One of them is an expert tracker. He
could smell your shit and tell you what you ate for
breakfast.'

The bank president recoiled slightly. Somehow
such language didn't go with a snappy suit, but
before he had time to comment, the detective continued at speed.

'It's a known fact that men on the dodge in this
part of the country usually make for the Indian
Territories, which means this gang will have to cross
the Arkansas River. And since it's both wide and
deep, they'll have to use a ferry and that means
they'll be seen. All we have to do is follow with firm
resolve and apprehend them. If they choose to resist,
then we'll kill every last one of the sons of bitches.
But believe me, Mister Clark, one way or another
your money is as good as recovered.'

The other man's eyes widened incredulously.
'You're a very confident young man, I'll give you that.'

Exley ignored the condescending tone. 'That's

because I'm very good at my job. And that's why I'm in charge of this operation.'

'Then I shall wait on results,' the banker replied. In spite of the situation he was beginning to feel a little happier. 'Is there anything I can do?'

'Yeah,' Exley drawled. 'Elect a new marshal!'

'If we were this close to the ferry, why did we sleep outdoors last night?' whined Jonas Bills.

He must have slept on a rock or some such, because his back was playing up something cruel. The two men had passed a quiet night, barely a mile from the river crossing. Mild weather and ample grazing for the horses meant that there had been little to complain of, unless you happened to be chained to a tree.

'Because door knocking in the dark is a sure way of getting my head blown off . . . and I'm kind of attached to it,' Sam Torrance responded, as he surveyed the tranquil scene before them. 'A lot of dangerous men use this trail and I've seen what John Taggart puts in his twelve gauge cartridges.'

At the bottom of a gentle incline lay a narrow stretch of flat land, bordered by the riverbank. A cabin and outbuildings were visible and beyond them flowed the Arkansas River. With a strong current, the waterway was anything but benign and definitely too much of a handful for any halfway rational horse and rider. Which, of course, explained the ferry tethered to a stout post. From that craft, there came the sound of honest labour, as a man in his early thirties deftly hammered nails into a new section of deck timber. The fact that he was missing his left arm didn't seem to affect his ability any.

As the two riders headed for the landing stage, a door banged in the cabin and a massively built individual strode purposefully into view. His sharp eyes took in the new arrivals and then he stopped and waited, hands on hips, for them to rein in next to him. His face wore a guarded smile, which suggested that he already knew one of the horsemen.

'Morning, marshal,' John Taggart remarked amiably. 'Who are you chasing this time?'

Torrance returned the smile. 'If I was to tell you that, you might just warn them.'

The ferry proprietor chuckled, but said nothing.

'You still charging one whole US Dollar per rider?'

Taggart nodded. 'That's the going rate. Round these parts, anyhow.' He glanced over at the manacled prisoner. 'You'd save Judge Parker a lot of time and trouble if you was to just tie him to a rock and heave him in the river. You could still claim the fare and nobody would know.'

As Bills noticeably paled, it was the lawman's turn to chuckle. 'You've got a real dark turn of mind, John Taggart. Problem is, it wouldn't work, because you and your partner over there would know and in any case, I've got a conscience. Maybe that's why I carry the law.'

There followed a long silence, as the two men eyed each other speculatively. It was the lawman who finally spoke. 'You had any customers recently?'

Taggart guffawed slightly. 'Now we're getting to it. How recently?'

'Today or maybe late on yesterday. There'd likely be six men, one of them wounded in the *left* shoulder.'

The big man shook his head decisively. 'Nope. Last ferrying business we had was early yesterday morning. Two fellas with pack mules heading south. Took them for whiskey peddlers or some such, out to rob and debauch the Indians. Not that I'd ever be able to recognize them again,' he added meaningfully. 'The wounded man . . . it wouldn't have been a .45-.75 cartridge, would it?'

The marshal smiled grimly. 'Yeah. It just so happened it was. They robbed a bank in Wichita and took off in this direction. I'd have bet cash money that they'd be in the Territories by now. Seems I was wrong.' He pondered for a moment. 'Do me a favour, John. If they should end up here, don't mention that I was asking about them, huh?'

Taggart nodded slowly. 'I reckon I can do that, but that's all I'll do. You know me, Sam. I earn my living ferrying all sorts of people across this river, so I don't ever inform on them. That way Jacob and I get to stay alive, savvy?'

Torrance favoured him with a lop-sided smile. 'I guess that's all any of us can hope for, John. Now how's about ferrying us across? This fellow has got a pressing appointment with the hangman.'

Jonas Bills scowled, but held his peace. He was sick and tired of being the butt of everyone's black humour. One way or another he was going to have to get clear of the federal law-dog.

'Better finish that later, Jacob,' Taggart called over to his partner. 'We've got us a couple of customers.'

That man carefully placed the hammer in his workbox and slid the barrier fully back to allow the animals access. 'You'll both need to dismount, marshal,' he announced sombrely. 'Ain't safe otherwise.'

Bills abruptly recognized an opportunity. 'For Christ's sake, marshal, give me a break from this saddle horn, huh? I feel like I'm married to it!'

Torrance glanced scathingly at him, but nevertheless released the manacle. Easing the prisoner off his horse, he then fastened the man's wrists behind his back and pushed him to the deck.

'You're all heart, marshal,' Bills muttered bleakly.

Taggart joined them on the craft and together the two ferrymen began to pull them across the Arkansas. Doing his best to compensate for the uneven motion, the lawman strolled over to the other side and glanced around. With a gentle breeze on his face and no effort required, it certainly was a very pleasant way to travel, if a bit unsettling at first. Unintentionally, his awareness began to drift. Not for the first time that year, he reflected that it really was time he started taking life a bit easier. A lawman's existence was all he knew, but it would be a sad thing indeed if that was to be his epitaph.

Regretfully, as with all nice things, the journey soon seemed to be over. The ferry reached the south bank, was made fast and the men and animals dis-embarked. Bills held his manacled hands well away from his body, making it easier for Torrance to reat-tach him to the saddle horn.

Vaguely uneasy, the marshal remarked, 'Not like you to be so co-operative.'

'Easier than having my shoulders wrenched out of joint,' came the snarling response, which as expected had the effect of allaying any doubt.

With both men back in their saddles, Marshal Torrance tipped his hat to the ferrymen. 'No doubt I'll see you fellas again afore long. Take it easy.' With that the horsemen rode off to the southeast. There was still a long way to go before they reached Fort Smith.

'You like that marshal, don't you, John?' Jacob remarked. It was more of a comment than a ques-tion, but Taggart found some words anyway.

'Yeah. Yeah I do. He's decent, which is more than can be said for most of the sour bellies that pass through here.'

The two men exchanged companionable smiles and then began to reverse their course across the river. With food now on their minds, it would be some considerable time before Jacob noticed that he had somehow misplaced his hammer!

'You know what all this means, don't you?'

Russ Decker glanced sharply at his sidekick. He knew exactly what was coming, but decided not to make it any easier. 'All what?'

Mark Lansing sighed with exasperation. 'The

Double Eagles of course and all those God damn letters! By taking those, we must have stirred up a real hornets' nest. We're bound to have every kind of law after us now.'

'What are you saying?' demanded Decker angrily. 'That I should have left that strongbox in the bank?'

Lansing nodded vigorously. 'Exactly that. And I said it at the time.'

The gang leader suddenly swung round in his saddle and made an abrupt checking motion towards their four companions. Since patching up Huey Soble, the gang had ridden hard, as Decker had decided that they needed after all to risk a dash for the river. As the bewildered horsemen came to a halt, their leader continued on with his subordinate until the two men were out of earshot. Ahead of them and now in plain sight, lay the Arkansas River, gleaming in the afternoon sun. Even though the winter rains were just a distant memory, it was still flowing fast. Far too fast to even consider crossing on horseback.

'In case you happen to have forgotten, we are bank robbers,' he remarked acidly. 'That means we rob banks and take *anything* in them. This time we've done good. Real good! And now it's up to me to keep us clear of anyone that would hang us. That's why I claim a larger share of any and all takings.' He momentarily paused to let that sink in. 'You're a good man, Mark, and a good friend, but you don't always see the bigger picture. We've finally got enough *dinero* to keep us in luxury and *señoritas* down in Mexico for years. And yet instead of treating me to a Daniel Webster cigar, all I get is bitch, bitch, bitch. Just think about it. All we have to do is make it there in one piece and we're made.'

In spite of his scepticism, Lansing couldn't help but be impressed. 'And I suppose you've got it all worked out.'

Decker nodded. 'You can bet your ass I have. We go south through the Indian Territories. Then roughly southwest across Texas and then turn south again into Mexico. It's a long, hard ride, but we can make it . . . well, maybe Huey won't. The key to it, is that we stop anyone from pursuing us past that river.'

'Even if it means more killing?' queried Lansing dubiously.

'That too,' his boss firmly replied. 'Is that a problem?'

'I guess I just wanted to know how this was all going to pan out,' the other man responded. 'We've been together a long time, Russ. I don't want to see us split up any time soon.'

Both men knew that he hadn't really answered the question, but Decker decided not to push it. Instead he made his intentions even plainer. 'So let's go put that ferry out of business . . . permanently!'

'What do you mean you've lost a hammer?' The question came out sharper than Taggart had intended and Jacob flinched.

'I guess it *could* have fallen over the side when we ferried the marshal across,' he replied nervously. 'I'm normally so careful, that's all.'

61

'I know you are,' the big man answered in a far milder tone. He was annoyed with himself, because he well knew that his friend couldn't handle any kind of stress. Then he spotted the six horsemen as they descended the gentle slope behind the cabin and he abruptly lost all interest in the missing tool. The fact that two men shared one animal gave him a clue as to what they might be. 'Happen it'll turn up,' he murmured distractedly.

The horses were well lathered, indicating that they had been ridden very hard. Despite the heat, all the men wore duster coats, except one who was very obviously injured . . . in the *left* shoulder.

'Looks like we've got some more customers,' Taggart remarked. 'Just remember, Jacob, Marshal Torrance was never here. Savvy? I've got a feeling that's as much for our benefit as his.'

The one-armed man nodded eagerly. Since that God-awful war, he hadn't been interested in what other people did, so long as they left him in peace. And in truth, he was still puzzling over the likely location of his hammer.

Leaving his injured companion to his thoughts, Taggart walked towards the newcomers. He consciously kept his features relaxed and greeted them affably enough. 'Howdy, friends. I'd say you all look ready to rest a spell. My ferry's a great place to watch the world go by, while somebody else does the work.'

The lead rider was a big man with sharp eyes. As he reined in, the others swiftly spread out to form a semi-circle around the ferryman. The move was obviously pre-planned to intimidate, but such tactics did not easily work with John Taggart and he held his ground.

'All in good time, mister. And that'll be my good time,' Decker replied. 'First off, I want to get my bearings. Tell me about this place. Who all's here apart from you and that amputee?'

Taggart bridled at the tone. He didn't care to hear such callous talk about his old comrade and also didn't take kindly to being railroaded on his own place. 'You'd better back up some, *friend*. We get all sorts of road agents and low-life's coming through here. What they learn, is that it's best just to quietly pay their dollar a piece and cross over, because sooner or later they're going to need us again.'

Russ Decker didn't like being referred to as a low-life. His right hand eased towards the long slit in his duster. Taggart noticed immediately and favoured him with a cold smile.

'There's also another fine reason to pay up. A .45-.75 cartridge will make a hell of a mess of a man at close range.'

That touched a collective nerve. As Decker's hand froze, Soble's pain-wracked eyes flitted nervously towards the cabin.

'I asked you before,' rasped the gang leader. 'Just who all else is on this spread?'

Taggart's response was uncompromising. 'You just don't get it, do you? This is my place and my rules. If you can't accept that, you'd better hightail it out of here and learn to swim!'

Decker could feel the blood pounding through his

veins and he drew in a deep breath to steady himself. He had told enough lies in his time to sense when someone was trying to humbug him. This big son of a bitch was really beginning to stick in his craw. He glanced over at Lansing as though seeking an opinion. His deputy merely offered an unhelpful shrug. So no comfort there then.

'Ok, if you want to run off at the mouth, let's do it by numbers,' the outlaw retorted. 'In my experience, such a rifle is going to belong to either a lawman or a buffalo hunter. Since there ain't any big shaggies left around here, that only leaves a law-dog.' Turning to face the cabin, he raised his voice. 'What are you, law-dog? Federal or local?'

Taggart began to edge casually over to the cabin door. 'You shouldn't ought to jump to conclusions, *friend.* It'll be the death of you one day.'

Suddenly so certain, Decker seized his holster gun and aimed it directly at the other man's head. There was no reaction from the cabin and so to hide his immense relief, he favoured the ferryman with a malicious grin. 'Seems like your friend must be asleep in there, or maybe you just like to play games, huh. Well do you?'

Although his bluff had been called, Taggart managed to maintain his confident demeanour. 'Only those that I win.'

The outlaw had heard enough. 'Mark, get his partner away from that ferry. We don't want it drifting away by *accident.*' Momentarily, he glanced over at his 'ramrod' and it was all the opening that John

Taggart needed.

Completely unexpectedly, the massive ferryman charged at Decker's horse, all the while bellowing at his partner. 'Jacob, get onto the river!'

Caught uncharacteristically off-guard, the gang leader tried to draw a bead, but his animal was in the way. As Jacob leapt onto the ferry and seized the cable, Taggart ducked down and grabbed Decker's right boot. With all his considerable strength, he hurled the outlaw clean out of the saddle and then taking the reins, used the animal as cover to reach his cabin.

As Decker hit the ground hard, his right index finger contracted. The sudden gunshot, although harmless, added to the brief confusion and spurred Jacob to greater efforts. Although desperately concerned over John's survival, he knew better than to ignore such a direct command and so heaved frantically on the heavy cable. Even though he still cursed the loss of his left arm, he did slowly but surely draw the craft away from the riverbank.

As Taggart slammed through the door of the cabin, one of the outlaws loosed off a shot at the ferry. Although gasping for breath, the gang leader still had full possession of his wits.

'Stop firing, you moron. How are we supposed to get the ferry back if he's dead?'

Inside the cabin, Taggart grabbed his cut down sawn-off and retracted both hammers. He knew full well that he couldn't kill all six desperados, but once the ferry was out of reach he would have a bargaining tool. Stepping to one side, he flung the door open and thrust his deadly weapon across the threshold. Unable to take aim, he just squeezed both triggers. There was a tremendous crash and his hand bucked under the recoil. Even through ringing ears, he could hear the tortured cries outside and they weren't all human.

Frantically, he ejected the smoking cartridges, but time was against him. Before he could load two fresh ones, the barrel of a revolver appeared directly before him. At the same time as the muzzle flash erupted towards his face, he felt a hammer blow on the side of his head and then everything went black.

Even over the noise of the mighty Arkansas, Jacob couldn't fail to recognize the distinctive sound of John's shotgun discharging. Unable to stop himself, he glanced back at the cabin. A horse and rider lay on the ground, both apparently twitching in their death throws, but that still left five more gunmen. Another shot rang out and despite the sweat pouring from his body, a dreadful chill swept over him. Surely his one and only friend in the world couldn't be dead.

Jonas Bills had waited hours for the right opportunity. His nerves were stretched to breaking point, because he knew he'd only get the one chance. That's all anybody ever got with Deputy US Marshal Sam Torrance. With his right hand securely manacled to the saddle, he needed the marshal on his left and close enough to touch. Ironically it was the lawman's basically decent nature that supplied the opportunity Bills desperately needed. Swinging in next to his unusually grim-faced prisoner, Torrance displayed a wedge of chewing tobacco.

'How's about a chaw? If you don't lighten up, you'll likely expire from a conniption fit before we even get to Fort Smith.'

Despite the pounding tension in his skull, Bills managed to present the makings of a grimace and nodded once.

'You really are all shit and no sugar,' replied the marshal, but nevertheless he produced a pocketknife and began to slice off a good-sized piece.

Bills eased his left hand out, as though to receive his unexpected present and then thrust it swiftly behind his back. His fingers closed around Jacob Stuckey's hammer and he dragged it out from under the rear of his jacket. Suddenly there could be no going back.

After years of hunting felons, Sam Torrance possessed a sixth sense for danger. Dropping the diminutive blade as though it were a hot coal, his right hand leapt for the revolver strapped to his waist. He very nearly made it!

The face of the hammer swung around in a wide arc and struck him squarely between the shoulder blades. Uttering a strangled cry, the federal officer tumbled forward off his horse and hit the ground with enough force to empty his lungs. With feverish anxiety, Bills slipped out of his saddle and lurched towards his victim, only to be painfully pulled up short by the unyielding manacle.

'God damn it to hell,' he snarled. Ignoring the sudden agony in his wrist, the crazed prisoner desperately dragged his animal nearer, but even then his bludgeon wouldn't quite reach the prone lawman. As Torrance began to draw air into his gasping lungs, the frustrated outlaw howled out a string of obscenities. Then it came to him . . . the cinch strap.

Frantically, he unbuckled the retaining belt and heaved the saddle to the ground. Like a maddened bear after its prey, Bills then dragged it across the 'tall and uncut' until he was directly above the recovering lawman. With great relish, the brutalized desperado swung out randomly at Torrance's heaving shoulders. Blow upon blow rained down on the defenceless man, until finally tiring of the sport Bills launched a great swipe at Torrance's skull. There was a shocking crack that surprised even the maniac responsible and his victim finally lay still.

'Hot dang,' whooped the outlaw jubilantly. 'I've actually done it. I've bested the son of a bitch!'

Surprised at his own success, Bills allowed the hammer to slip from his grasp as he dropped to his knees next to the undoubtedly dead lawman. After a moment's hesitation, he eagerly rifled Torrance's pockets of anything and everything. The discovery of the key to the manacles brought a grunt of satisfaction, soon followed by an exhilarating sense of freedom as the shackle permanently fell away.

After briefly massaging his wrist, Bills heaved the marshal over onto his back and unbuckled the black leather gun belt. 'Haw, haw, haw,' he crowed to the empty landscape, as he strapped the quality acquisition around his own waist. Still not quite able to believe his own good fortune, the outlaw suddenly glanced nervously down at the unmoving lawman.

'Treated me like dirt, didn't you? You old bastard,' he shouted out. Then, for some unaccountable reason, the outlaw felt a chill come over him. It was like a sixth sense warning him that he was no longer alone. Quite unexpectedly under the circumstances, he had a sudden overwhelming urge to be on his way . . . fast.

No longer burdened by a saddle, Bills' horse had wandered off in search of grazing and he had no inclination to go after it. The marshal's animal would serve well enough and besides, it had that top-notch Winchester in its saddle scabbard. Any God damned posse had better watch out, now that he possessed such a weapon.

Consciously shaking off the strange sense of unease that had gripped him, he pocketed all his booty and clambered to his feet. Without giving Jacob's hammer a second thought, Jonas Bills mounted up and quickly rode away. With an instinctive desire to keep well clear of Fort Smith, he headed west: deeper into the Indian Territories.

CHAPTER SIX

The seven men had left town at a gallop, but that was just to put on a show for the bank president who Ben Exley knew would be watching. Once out of sight of the rooftops, the Pinkerton Agents had reined back to a steady walk. Although the trail was over a day old, Exley had no intention of running his men ragged. Apart from anything else, he didn't need to. Even a small child could point the way to the Arkansas River and once beyond that he had Raoul.

The Pinkerton glanced over at his tracker and grunted to himself. Of all the men that he had encountered in his eventful life, no one had possessed the capacity to unnerve him quite like Raoul. Exley thought of the man as a half-breed, but in truth his ancestry was probably far more varied than that. For a start, his name was French, which suggested that one of his forebears had been a fur trapper or some such. He had sallow skin and eyes like black coals that were never still. A vicious quirt dangled from his left wrist, which Exley had once seen used to lash a man into blubbering submission. Time and again throughout the mid-west, Raoul had proven his worth in hunting down bank and train robbers.

It was said that only an Indian could track another Indian, but they weren't hunting redskins and so one thing was a certainty. If those God damned murdering thieves had crossed over into the Nations, then Raoul would find them!

Jacob Stuckey lay flat out on the ferry's timber decking. It didn't occur to him that the last thing the outlaws might want was for him to be dead and feeding the fish. The craft was more or less stationary, some few yards away from the south bank. That way he was able to avoid the buffeting of the main current, but could not be surprised by anyone coming out of the Indian Territories. He was trembling with anxiety over the condition of his friend and the situation was only compounded by his enforced inactivity. And yet, he was obeying John's last command to 'get onto the river' and so far nothing had happened to change the good sense in that.

Russ Decker stared down at the big bastard and cursed fluently. Thanks to him they had one man paroled to Jesus and the ferry exactly where it shouldn't be. Taggart deserved to be dead, but fortunately he wasn't. He had actually been incredibly lucky. The bullet had grazed his skull and his face was mottled with powder burns, but he had survived to be of some use to his attackers.

'Heave some river water over the son of a bitch

and get him on his feet,' the outlaw ordered.

As one of his men hurried off to comply, the gang leader turned towards Lansing. 'If this turns into a stand-off, we'll be the losers by it. There has to be some kind of posse looking for us and we sure as hell can't get across that river without the ferry. Even if we risked it and spread the gold across the five of us, it's odds on we'd lose some in that current.'

His sidekick regarded him thoughtfully. 'So we blow bits off of him until his partner brings the ferry back, is that it?'

Despite the situation, Decker laughed out loud. 'For a youngster you catch on quick, don't you?'

Lansing grunted unhappily. 'I wish I was still a young un. I'd tread a different path and that's no error.'

His boss regarded him darkly. He really was beginning to have doubts about his commitment, but now wasn't the time to provoke a confrontation.

At that moment, a bucket of chill water descended on Taggart's smarting features and he coughed and spluttered on the floor of the cabin. As the liquid flowed off him, it was tinged with blood from where the bullet had creased his skull. With his eyes open and wits returning, the ferry operator glanced around until his gaze fastened onto Russ Decker. Anger was evident, but there was something else as well. They were the eyes of an intelligent man and that made him dangerous.

'You can glare at me all you want, big man,' Decker snarled. 'But right now, we're holding all the aces *and* all the guns, so walk softly.'

'Not *all* the aces,' Taggart responded quickly. 'Otherwise I'd be dead and you low-lifes would be over in the Nations.'

Decker's eyes narrowed menacingly. That was the second time he'd been directly referred to as a low-life and the experience hadn't improved any. 'All right, you. Get vertical and step outside. Keep your guns on him, boys. This here's a *real* dangerous man.'

Silently and unaided, Taggart staggered to his feet. He stood for a few moments, unhindered by his captors, but swaying slightly until his head cleared. Only then did he venture across the threshold. Before him lay the mighty Arkansas. His ferry waited close to the far side and his heart momentarily lurched when he couldn't immediately spot Jacob. Then he noticed his partner's horizontal figure on the deck and he smiled with relief. That satisfaction proved to be short lived. A gun muzzle was suddenly pressed against the side of his head and he heard the distinctive double click of the hammer being cocked.

'You with the one arm,' Decker bellowed out. 'If you value your friend's life, you'd better get that ferry back here, pronto. Otherwise I'm going to turn his head into a canoe. Savvy?'

Minutes passed and the question hung in the air unanswered, until at last the outlaw leader hissed in Taggart's ear. 'Did he lose his tongue along with his arm, or does he just want you dead?'

The big man turned his head slightly against the pressure of the revolver. 'That damned war changed him. It affected his mind as much as his body. Why not let me talk to him? He trusts me.'

The outlaw stared at him for a long moment, before finally nodding slowly. 'I guess it can't hurt. But no tricks, or it'll end badly for both of you.'

Returning his gaze to his prone partner, Taggart drew in a deep breath. He was very conscious that what he said next could get them both killed. 'Jacob, you hear me?'

The response was instantaneous. 'I hear you, John. What have I to do?'

'I know you're a mite short-handed at the moment,' the big man responded. There were chuckles around him, as he had anticipated and the pressure on his head eased slightly. 'If you remember what those two *Union* sons of bitches left behind, you might want to make use of them.'

Jacob raised his head slightly, as though searching for something and then nodded sharply. Without any warning, he rolled rapidly to the side of the ferry, sucked in a deep breath and simply dropped over-board. There was a splash and momentary thrashing in the water and then . . . nothing.

'What the hell just happened?' Decker bellowed out. His men were completely non-plussed, except for Mark Lansing who favoured the ferryman with a shrewd glance.

'I think Russ was right,' he commented softly. 'You are dangerous.'

The outlaw boss took a step backward and then viciously pistol-whipped Taggart across his face.

74

Strong as he was, no one could resist that kind of blow and down he went. The big man was again on the ground and defenceless and this time it was Decker who took deliberate aim at him. With the muzzle pointing directly at Taggart's bleeding face, he squeezed the trigger.

As Jacob Stuckey dropped below the surface, he gasped with shock. It might have been summer, but the water was still damned cold. Reaching out with his one hand, he heaved his body under the ferry and stayed there for a moment, resisting the tug of the current as he got his bearings. Then, knowing what had to be done, he kicked out strongly to propel himself deeper. Although disabled and traumatized, Jacob was also robust and determined and under orders from the only man he trusted in the world. He soon reached the river bottom. It was probably for the best that he didn't hear the single gun shot that crashed out in front of the cabin. As it was, he used his legs to help remain on the bottom and desperately searched for the discarded weapons.

Mark Lansing's hand struck the revolver barrel just at the moment of discharge. As the bullet slammed into earth barely an inch from his head, Taggart's battered features received mild burns from the muzzle flash. By now his face resembled a charred steak, but at least he was still alive. Decker was beside himself with anger.

'What the hell's wrong with you?' he barked at Lansing. 'But for this pus weasel, we'd all be across that river by now!'

His deputy sighed wearily. 'He was only trying to protect what's his. And besides, what's done is done, but if a posse should find us with yet another dead citizen it'd likely go badly for us.' He paused, before adding, 'You reckon?'

Decker silently glared at him whilst absorbing the unwanted advice, before finally acknowledging that the moment for killing had passed . . . at least temporarily. 'You want him, you got him. Have him tied up and out of my sight.' Holstering his weapon, he returned his attention to the abandoned ferry. 'Looks like he don't figure on returning and time's moving on. If that thing's not coming to us, then we'll have to go and get it. Seems as though someone's set to get wet!'

Jacob knew that he could not last much longer. His chest was tight. His head pounded from a lack of oxygen. Frantically he groped around on the river bottom. They had to be here. They just *had* to be. Then he felt it. A buckle. Elatedly, he seized the gun belt. Possessing only one hand, he was unable to strap it on and so instead rammed one end of the belt deep into the crotch of his trousers. His lungs felt as though they must surely burst. Recovering two rifles was out of the question, but then his searching fingers found the other holstered revolver and he knew that he had done enough. It was time to surface.

Peering up at the ferry's solid bulk, Jacob kicked out at the riverbed and even with the extra weight rapidly shot to the surface. His head cleared water just behind the timber craft, so that he was hidden from the far shore. Gratefully he sucked fresh air into his burning lungs. The relief was tremendous and, for some considerable while, breathing was all that concerned him. Then he got to thinking about what to do next. One way or another, he had to find a way to help John and that meant remaining close to the ferry. And yet to climb up the bank behind him was to invite discovery.

Very reluctantly, Jacob drew in one last deep breath and again dropped below the surface. Swimming with the current, he headed downstream until his chest began to hurt again. With weakness beginning to overwhelm him, he veered immediately towards the bank. Then, facing the sky, he tilted his head back so that only his face was out of the water. Breathing deeply, he carefully scrutinized the far bank. Jacob was now nearly one hundred yards away from his ferry and no one was watching anyway. Two of the outlaws seemed to be helping his friend back into the cabin, so at least John was still alive. Greatly encouraged by that, he decided to get out of the river.

Using the plentiful vegetation as cover, the ferry-man was soon hidden in the undergrowth well back from the river. Accepting that he would have to remain in wet clothes, he dropped to the ground and awkwardly buckled on one of the gun belts. Thankfully, they were cartridge revolvers rather than cap 'n ball, so there was a good chance that the powder would not be spoiled. It was only then that it dawned on him that to help his friend he might actually have to shoot somebody. The deep chill that suddenly assailed him had nothing to do with his unexpected swim, but to counter it he got to his feet and began walking back towards the abandoned ferry.

'Brett, get back up that trail a short way and keep watch,' Decker ordered. 'Any movement, come tell me. And *no* shooting, you hear?'

The fair-haired bank robber nodded eagerly and turned away. He was glad to be gone. Whatever his boss was planning was likely to involve water and he didn't swim too well. In fact he couldn't swim at all, but didn't care to admit it.

With Huey Soble resting his throbbing arm on a cot in the cabin and the other remaining outlaw securely binding Taggart, only Decker and his deputy were left by the landing stage. The gang boss's expression was grim.

'One of us has got to bring that ferry back,' he announced, staring pointedly at Lansing.

That man frowned. He wasn't for a moment fooled by 'one of us' and so snapped back. 'Why me? What about Josh? In fact, come to think of it, what about you?'

It was Decker's turn to scowl. 'All Josh is good for is frightening women and children. Oh, and back shooting. We don't know for sure that that fella over there has hightailed it for good. I need someone with at least half a brain to haul that ferry back. Without it, we're all in trouble.' He paused as though recollecting something. 'And *I'm* not doing it, because I need to be here in case some posse turns up looking for a fight. Savvy?'

Lansing sighed. Oh he savvied, all right. Deep down, he knew that this was really about Decker reasserting his authority and also testing to see if his 'side kick's' heart was still in it. And in truth it really wasn't any more, but nevertheless something stirred inside of Mark Lansing. He had been presented with an unmistakeable challenge that had awakened his stubborn streak. It was going to take more than any river and a one-armed man to stop him getting to Mexico!

As Jacob watched the lone figure slip into the water from the landing stage, he began to tremble with apprehension. He now had more weapons than he could physically use, but the prospect of having to fire one filled him with gnawing anxiety. He would remember, until his dying day, the unremitting agony as the army surgeon's blood-soaked saw bit into his mangled left arm. The damage had been caused by a spinning Minie Ball from the rifle of a Union soldier and ever since, he had lived in dread of having to get into another firefight. And yet, as he watched the outlaw dragging himself hand over hand across the Arkansas, Jacob recognized that he would just have to damn well control his fear.

Lansing soon realized that without the thick cable, his chances of crossing the fast-flowing river would have been slim indeed and Slim had just left town. His brief chuckle at the tired jest was abruptly halted by a mouthful of water. It was also dawning on him that heaving the heavy craft back across the river was going to be mighty hard toil. Then again, if someone with only one arm could do it, then he surely could. And what of the one-armed ferryman? Had he really permanently vamoosed? It seemed unlikely. He just hoped that Decker was making good his promise to cover him with a Winchester.

Jacob blinked nervously as he spotted the marksman on the far bank. The only thing preventing him from turning tail was the sure knowledge that John needed him. Desperately trying to control his fear, he drew and cocked his newly acquired revolver. The other gunbelt was coiled up back in the undergrowth, for use as a holdout weapon. Crouching low, he moved stealthily through the vegetation, ensuring that he kept the ferry between him and the rifleman. The approaching outlaw had almost reached the craft. It seemed as though some kind of confrontation was unavoidable.

Mark Lansing was tiring. His arms felt like dead weights. He wasn't used to such physical exertion. Thankfully, he was barely two yards from the ferry, but the cable ran up out of the water towards it. This meant that to avoid letting go and running the risk of being swept downriver, he would need to haul himself bodily out of the water. If there were anyone waiting for him, that was when he would be most vulnerable. Breathlessly, he paused for a moment in the chill water and rapidly glanced back. That son of a bitch had better be there!

Jacob watched intently as the soaking wet figure

wearily reached for the timber railing. If he was going to do this thing, then it had to be now whilst the other man was clinging on with both hands. And because of the stretch of river between them, his only option was to use the threat of his Colt. Mouth dry with fear, he clambered to his feet and rushed forward.

'Jump back in the river and go with the current or I'll fire,' he shouted. 'Please!'

Horrified at the sudden apparition, Lansing momentarily froze. With a great flood of relief, Jacob decided that everything was going to be all right after all. There would be no shooting and no horrific wounds to contend with.

Russ Decker watched as his man finally reached the ferry. If anything were going to happen, it would be now. After levering up a cartridge out of the tubular magazine, he tucked the 'Yellow Boy' Winchester into his shoulder and waited impatiently . . . but not for long. As Lansing had dragged himself out of the river, there was movement in the bushes on the far bank. It looked like the one-armed man, but Decker could not be sure because his damned sidekick was in the way.

'Move, you son of a bitch,' he angrily murmured and then fired anyway.

The bullet slammed into the timber railing a short distance beyond Lansing's weary body. It was far nearer to him than to Decker's intended victim and so very definitely had the effect of spurring Lansing into action. Dropping to his knees on the decking, he grabbed for his revolver.

Jacob watched that dreaded act with dismay. He now had to do what he had so desperately hoped to avoid. Rapidly drawing a bead on the other man's torso, he squeezed the trigger. Instead of the expected detonation, there was merely a dull click. The river water had done its work. *Misfire!*

Lansing couldn't believe his luck, but now he had to profit from it. His right hand closed around the butt of his revolver and he swiftly levelled it at his assailant. Yet when he tried to thumb back the hammer, the river water worked against him as well. At the first attempt, his digit simply slid off the metal.

Jacob had no such problem. Again he cocked and squeezed and this time the Colt blasted out its deadly load. The heavy bullet struck Lansing in the soft flesh of his belly. He let out a tremendous groan, released his hold on the rail and dropped painfully to his knees. It was that last action that saved him from falling back into the river.

As Decker watched his man collapse, he swore violently and began to work the Winchester's lever action like a maniac. Bullet after bullet sped across the Arkansas, until he was enveloped in such a cloud of acrid smoke that he could no longer see.

'What in tarnation's happening, boss?' yelled Josh from the cabin's entrance.

'I fancied a nice buffalo tongue,' Decker responded acidly. 'What the hell d'you think's happening, you moron? Get back inside.'

Stepping clear of the powder smoke, he anxiously

peered across the river. Lansing was still on his knees, but now doubled over. Of the ferryman there was no sign, but that didn't mean he was dead.

'Mark,' he bellowed out. 'Can you hear me?'

For a moment there was no response, but then the other man slowly raised his left hand to shoulder height before allowing it to drop like a lead weight.

Grunting, Decker continued with, 'Is that one-armed cockchafer still alive? I *need* to know!'

The answer, when it came, was bitterly disappointing and hard to swallow. Lansing made no response, but there was sudden movement in the bushes and a gunshot rang out. The bullet came nowhere near, but then a new voice rang out across the water.

'Don't send anyone else across, *please*,' Jacob pleaded from the safety of cover. 'I really don't want to hurt anyone.'

'You've got a funny way of showing it,' Decker retorted indignantly. He stood for a moment and pondered. 'So what about my man there? What happens to him?'

'I'll do what I can for him, but you stay well clear. You hear?'

Decker glanced down at the little pile of empty cartridges that seemed to mock his apparent impotence. 'Great,' he snarled. 'Just great!' Turning, he stormed off towards the cabin, pausing only to hurl out, 'You bull turd. I'm going to have your other arm before this is all over!'

Arriving back in the cabin, he peered wildly at Josh and Huey. 'It'll be night time soon,' he announced.

'We'll have to fort up here until I can figure out what to do next.'

Huey, still in great pain, stared at him aghast. 'That's a plan?'

CHAPTER SEVEN

Jonas Bills detected the smell of food long before he saw it and it made his guts ache. The sun was going down and he had covered a lot of miles since slaying the marshal. Not wanting to build a fire of his own, he had made do with cold beef jerky and corn dodgers from the lawman's saddle-bags. It was not surprising then, that the aroma of sizzling bacon was more than he could endure.

Cautiously cresting a low rise, he spotted a small stand of trees in the middle distance. A single horse grazed in plain view, whilst its owner, partially concealed by foliage, was hunched over a campfire with his back to the hungry outlaw. Light from the flames danced in the encroaching branches. It was an idyllic scene, made more attractive by the fact that yet again he would be able to get something for nothing.

Bills' lean features twisted into a grin as he extracted his brutally acquired Winchester from its scabbard. He chambered a cartridge and drew a bead on the unsuspecting figure. On the point of squeezing the trigger, he was suddenly assailed by unaccustomed caution. He knew for a fact that he was deep in Creek Indian Territory. Although known as one of the five 'civilized' tribes, he recalled people said that they weren't always that civilized. Better to leave gunfire as a last resort.

Retaining his grip on the rifle, Bills cautiously urged his mount towards the trees, all the while checking the terrain around him. As he drew closer, the lone stranger glanced around in apparent surprise and slowly got to his feet. He was a big-boned fellow with an unkempt beard who, to Bills' startled eyes, possessed one very notable redeeming feature. He appeared to be completely unarmed, which in itself begged a question. What fool would travel through Indian country without even so much as a belt gun?

'Hello the fire,' the outlaw called out with a modest attempt at bonhomie. 'That bacon's been working on my guts for the last mile. What say I help you finish it?'

The bearded man glanced briefly at the Winchester. Then his hairy features broke into a smile. 'Hell, you won't need to bully me with that long gun, friend. There's more than enough to go around and it'll be nice to have some company.'

Bills weighed up the other man suspiciously. He wasn't used to folks being nice to him. 'So say you,' he gruffly replied. 'But I'll be happier with some space between us. Back off!'

The other man frowned briefly, but nevertheless

retreated further into the wood. His demeanour indicated acceptance, rather than anger or fear. If Bills hadn't been so hungry, he might have pondered on that. Instead, he merely dismounted and advanced into the welcoming shade. It momentarily crossed his mind to scrutinize the branches above, but with rashers of bacon sizzling temptingly in a pan, it was more than he could do to tear his eyes away from them.

'Down on the ground,' he barked impatiently. 'Sit on your hands and if you're lucky I might let you live.'

To his great surprise, his captive merely grinned at him. Then a sudden rustling of foliage came from directly above and Jonas Bills was gripped by an all too familiar icy chill. Desperately, he tried to step back and raise his rifle, but before he had time to do either, a dead weight crashed onto his shoulders and sent him tumbling to the grass.

Winded and pinned to the ground, he had no chance to react before six inches of honed steel penetrated between his ribs. As his lifeblood unstoppably erupted over the greenery, any chance of resistance disappeared. In fact, despite the shocking agony, the stricken outlaw wasn't even able to cry out. Time and again the vicious blade ferociously pierced the soft flesh of his torso. Jonas Bills twitched violently and then died without even knowing the identity of his assailant. It was a sad fact that under different circumstances he would definitely have approved of such savagery.

As his kill crazy lust finally abated, the scrawny assassin with the thin moustache got slowly to his feet and backed away from his blood-drenched victim.

'Jesus, Klee,' the bearded individual exclaimed. 'Remind me never to let you get to the back of me with a knife!'

'Huh, that was too easy,' Klee remarked scornfully, as he glanced curiously over at the discarded rifle lying in the grass. He briefly hunkered down to clean his blade on Bills' trousers, before moving off to claim his prize. Eyes widening with unexpected delight, he gleefully grasped the strongly constructed Winchester and proclaimed, 'Will you look at this gun? It sure beats the hell out of my old Spencer. You could bring down a grizzly with it and not even break into a sweat.'

The other man registered annoyance. 'I kind of thought that'd be mine. On account of I'm smarter and this was all my idea.'

Klee's tight lips twisted into a sneer. 'Too thin, Brad, too thin. You could have written the Gettysburg Address for old Abe, but this still wouldn't be yourn. I drew blood for it, which makes me entitled.'

'Yeah, yeah,' muttered Brad sourly, but nevertheless he made no further objection. Instead he ambled over to the cadaver and unbuckled the shiny gun belt. 'I guess I'll just have to settle for this smoke wagon. At least we're toting some firearms at last.'

The smaller man nodded thoughtfully. 'Which means we can go settle scores with that bastard Taggart and his armless Reb. Funny thing though. These weapons look too classy by far for that stiff. He looked down on his luck, even before I put all those holes in him.' With that, he headed off through the trees to collect his own horse, which had been tethered out of sight along with the two heavily laden pack mules.

Brad watched him leave through narrowed eyes. He didn't give a damn who their new weapons had once belonged to, but one thing was for sure. He definitely didn't like deferring to anyone and it occurred to him that there might have to be another reckoning once the big ferryman had cashed in his chips! That way, the sale proceeds of their newly acquired horse and saddle wouldn't have to be diluted by any unnecessary 50/50 split. Not to mention all the cheap trader whiskey that they were still hauling around!

Very tentatively, Sam Torrance opened his eyes and immediately regretted it. He was lying on his back and so what remained of the day's light seemed to lance in to every corner of his pain-wracked skull. Groaning, he snapped his eyelids shut and tried to make sense of his parlous situation. All he could remember was offering Jonas Bills some chewing tobacco. Somehow or other, the 'bull turd' must have got the drop on him and left him for dead.

Keeping his eyes closed, the marshal gingerly ran trembling hands over his body. Gun belt gone, naturally. Money gone, but thankfully he still seemed to possess his boots, because it was highly likely that he would be on foot.

'God damn it all to hell,' he snarled angrily. His pride appeared to have come off worse than his body and so, very recklessly, Torrance rolled onto one side as a prelude to getting up. Terrifyingly, a section of bone seemed to shift very unpleasantly under his scalp and he howled out with pain and shock. As nausea threatened to overwhelm him, the lawman realized that there was something badly wrong with his head. He had pistol-whipped enough felons in his time to know that he very likely had a fractured skull.

At that point, most other mortals would have succumbed to self-pity and stayed put for a time, but that wasn't his way. Gritting his teeth, he continued with the roll until he was on hands and knees. It was then that he discovered that his shoulders had also taken a severe pounding. That pus weasel Jonas Bills had certainly exacted a heavy toll.

For long moments, the battered federal officer remained almost immobile, just breathing slow and deep. Then, with eyes wide open, he made a supreme effort and clambered unsteadily to his feet. Something seemed to explode inside his head and he let out a tremendous groan . . . *but* he did remain upright. Noticeably swaying, Torrance made no attempt to move. He just stood there and allowed his narrowed eyes to scrutinize his surroundings.

To his great delight, the first thing that he saw was Jonas Bills' horse. His heart momentarily sank when he realised that he would have to saddle it, but then he noticed something else that brought a scowl of bitter anger to his features. On the grass, barely three feet away, lay a solitary hammer. Realising full well its dark purpose, Torrance decided there and then that whatever effort it cost him, he would be taking it with him. But where to go? Logic dictated a return to Taggart's Crossing. He knew that when the chips were down, the big man would help him in any way possible . . . always supposing that he was able to, of course. There were definite limits to what any amateur sawbones could achieve.

It took him a horrendous amount of time and much painful effort to saddle the reluctant animal. Every part of his upper body seemed to hurt and his mood wasn't improved by the discovery of the manacles still fastened to the saddle horn. Since the key was nowhere to be seen, they would be a constant reminder of the dreadful change in his circumstances.

Although night was beginning to fall, the marshal decided that he had spent enough time in one place. He was effectively unarmed and his surroundings weren't known as the Indian Territories for nothing. Steeling himself against the inevitable pain, Sam Torrance took hold of the saddle horn and dragged his pain-wracked body up into the saddle. It was more than he could do not to cry out and even when mounted it was some time before he was able to urge the horse forward. He decided there and then to only travel until full darkness had descended. In his condition, it made no sense to risk a tumble that he most likely wouldn't get up from. And so it was that he began the slow and painful journey back to the *safety* of Taggart's Crossing.

Unable to ignore the man's desperate pleas, Jacob had reluctantly entered the water again. Fetching up on the ferry brought him face to face with his gutshot victim and he wasn't a pretty sight. The surrounding timber was stained with blood . . . a lot of it. Under the present circumstances, or indeed any other imaginable, the bullet was untouchable and death inevitable. All he could do was maybe bind the wound and make him as comfortable as possible. Then his common sense told him that any attempt to tinker would only generate unnecessary agony. Considering his usual reticence, Jacob was remarkably forthright.

'I cain't do nothing for you, mister,' he softly announced, as he scooped up yet another discarded revolver from the deck before him. 'I know you're outlawed up, but I'm real sorry it's come to this.'

Mark Lansing had seen enough death to know what was coming his way. He nodded silently and then reached out to touch Jacob's leg. 'I guess I had it coming eventually. Just stay with me for a while, huh? I don't want to leave this world all on my lonesome.'

His killer pondered that request for a moment. It was a big ask. Remaining on the ferry made him vulnerable to another attack. Then again, the light had almost gone and only a fool would try to cross that river in darkness. 'I reckon I can stay with you for a while,' he responded. 'Just don't try anything. Yeah?'

Lansing attempted a chuckle, but it came out as a groan. 'Mister, my trying days are all over.' He paused for a painful moment, before continuing with, 'I'm powerful thirsty all of a sudden.'

Jacob laughed spontaneously. 'Well I'll tell you, water's *one* thing we're not short of hereabouts.'

John Taggart lay uncomfortably on the hard floor, apparently forgotten about for the moment. His cot, built to accommodate an outsize frame, had been requisitioned by the wounded outlaw known as Huey. Decker had taken Jacob's, although he was currently pacing up and down the room, deep in thought. With darkness having fallen, Brett had returned to the cabin and now stood drinking Taggart's coffee, for all the world as though he owned the place. He was content to let someone else do all the thinking, but one of his companions was far less complacent. Despite, or maybe because of his being in pain, Huey was about to go on the prod.

'Way I see it, boss, we're caught between a rock and a hard place. So what are *you* gonna do about it?'

The outlaw leader came to a grinding halt. His grim expression and blazing eyes indicated that he was on a very short fuse indeed. And as Decker's right hand moved fractionally towards the holstered Colt, Huey belatedly contemplated the prospect of another bullet wound. It therefore took everybody by surprise when Decker suddenly transferred his full attention to the bound ferryman.

'Come daylight, it's make or break time, big man. You're going back out there under my gun again. Only this time if that limbless son of a bitch doesn't bring the ferry back, I'll take you apart piece by piece. It ain't just Indians that know how to torment a man.' Without awaiting a response, he abruptly returned his fierce gaze to the wounded outlaw. 'That's *my* plan. Take it or leave it, *hombre*,' he hissed.

CHAPTER EIGHT

Brett had been ensconced on the reverse slope of the rise above the cabin for just over one hour and on such a summer's morning it was definitely no hardship. In truth, he was glad to be clear of Russ Decker, who ever since their arrival at the ferry crossing had been behaving like a bear with a sore head. And yet his temporary independence was about to go sour. A group of seven riders suddenly came into view, heading at a steady pace from the direction of Wichita. They had all the appearance of a posse, which of course was exactly what they were.

'Oh shit,' he muttered unhappily. Chambering a cartridge in his old Henry, Brett abruptly had an unwelcome decision to make. Should he open fire or hightail it back to Decker for instructions? Recognizing that the horsemen had to be kept clear of the cabin, he decided on the former. Tucking the well-worn butt into his shoulder, the outlaw drew a bead on the leading rider.

The Pinkerton men had been in the saddle since

daybreak. They all knew that the river was close, but it was Raoul riding point who saved someone's life . . . quite possibly his own. Without warning, he brutally reined in and slid from the saddle. Expertly, he pulled his horse to the ground and dropped down over its neck, rifle in hand. His startled companions were seasoned detectives. They well understood what such action meant and knew better than to question his judgment. After rapidly dismounting, five of them handed their reins to a single horse holder who backed off with six mounts, leaving the other men to spread out across the trail.

Ben Exley called over to the tracker. 'What's got you spooked, Raoul?' His unfortunate word choice indicated that he had definitely been taken by surprise.

'*Nothing* spooks me. You well know that, *Mister* Exley,' came the snarling retort. 'Somebody has us under his gun, is all.'

'I don't see nothing,' retorted one of the others.

'That don't mean shit,' Raoul responded scathingly. 'It's enough that I know he's out there.'

Exley nodded his agreement. 'You've always been right before, so I'll go with that. What do you propose?'

'I'll move in to flush him out. He'll either open fire or hightail it. And if you start shooting, just remember that I'm in front of you, yeah?' Without waiting for a response, he imperiously added, 'One of you get over here and lie on this horse. He don't get paid enough to risk a bullet.' With this achieved, the 'breed crawled off through the long grass without another word.

Brett had observed the posse's rapid dispersal with incredulity. He couldn't work out how they had spotted him, but the sure knowledge that they had, began to work on his nerves. Sweaty palms ran in his family and they were sure as hell running now. As the posse's point man stealthily advanced towards him, the bank robber knew that it was time to retreat. Staying low, he slid back down the gentle rise before racing over to the cabin.

'It's Brett. I'm coming in,' he had the sense to yell, before running at the door. Bursting inside in a state of feverish anxiety, he found three weapons levelled at him. 'Sweet Jesus, don't shoot, fellas. It's not me you need to worry over, but that damned posse.'

Decker leapt forward and literally grabbed him by the throat. 'How many and what kind of law?'

Brett shook himself free. 'Hell, don't take on at me, boss,' he whined. 'There's maybe half a dozen or so. From the way they went to ground, I reckon they're professionals, not local law or cowmen making up the numbers.'

'Just great,' Decker muttered, suddenly deep in thought. He wasn't long in coming to a decision. 'OK, so we knew this would happen. Josh. Get back up there with him. And you too, Huey. I know you're hurting, but I can't spare you. The three of you have got to hold them off while I get that ferry back on side. You hear me? Whatever it takes, just keep them away from the landing stage.' With that, he switched his full attention to John Taggart.

The ferryman had passed a poor night on the hard floor. His hands and feet remained bound and his face was blistered and sore from the two near misses. Yet his eyes glittered in a way that suggested he still had plenty of fight left in him.

As the three outlaws left the cabin, Decker unsheathed his hunting knife and sliced through the rope around his prisoner's legs. 'On your feet, you big bastard. I let you live last night. Now you're going to earn it.'

Despite his natural belligerence, Taggart was unable to stifle a moan as he staggered to his feet. With circulation returning, the pain in his legs was truly murderous. As Decker impatiently shoved him towards the threshold, Huey abruptly re-appeared. The suspicion on his face was plain to see.

'You'll be sure an' let us know when you're ready to leave, won't you, boss? Only you'll likely need help carrying all those gold coins into the Nations.'

The inference was obvious and Decker didn't like it one bit. 'When I side with a man, I stick with him,' he responded angrily. 'I don't cheat him and I don't leave him to the buzzards ... like we could have done with you. Now get back up that hillside and help the others!'

The outlaw scowled, but finally did as he was told. Hefting the Winchester in his left hand, Decker drew his revolver and prodded his captive outside. 'Get over to the landing stage. Let's see if that friend of yours is awake yet.'

When the two men reached the riverbank, Decker

kicked out sharply at the back of Taggart's right leg. That man groaned and dropped to his knees as intended.

'Mark. You still with us?' the outlaw bellowed out. The jarring response was a volley of gunshots crashing out from behind the cabin. A gunfight was only to be expected but not what he had hoped for and served to highlight just how perilous their situation had quickly become.

'God damn it, answer me,' he persisted. 'I ain't got all day.'

Over on the ferry, Jacob crouched down in front of the lifeless body. The unexpected outbreak of gunfire had only added to the pressure on his already troubled mind. He had passed a thoroughly uncomfortable night, looking on helplessly as his victim died a lingering and painful death. The experience had brought back vivid memories of the seemingly all too recent war. He felt scarred and troubled. If John Taggart's survival hadn't been at stake, he would have swum ashore and simply left. On foot. Anywhere. As it was, he couldn't indulge in such futile luxury.

Keeping low, Jacob reached over and slowly lifted Lansing's left arm. Raising it enough to be noticed on the far bank, he then let it drop and partially showed himself.

'That's the best you're going to get,' he replied. 'Your friend is in a bad way. He'll need a doctor and some good vittles if he's ever going to ride with you again.'

Decker sighed unhappily. The firing behind him showed no sign of lessening and his patience was wearing thin. 'Never mind all that. I've dusted your compadre down and brought him out to try again. I'm a reasonable man, but you've tested my tolerance. I want that ferry brought back here, now. *Otherwise*, I'll cripple this son of a bitch for life. I reckon you'll know how that feels,' he added gratuitously.

Considering that he was surrounded by fresh water, Jacob's mouth began to grow uncomfortably dry. It was years since he had felt so terrified and helpless in equal measure. And yet, that damned war *had* taught him a thing or two. Most battles at some point rely on bluff. Drawing his revolver, he cocked it and then pointed it directly at Lansing's lifeless skull.

'You harm John in any way and I'll shoot your friend,' Jacob called back, somehow managing to sound far more threatening than he actually felt. 'I've killed before, so you'd better believe I'll do it.'

Sadly, his enemy's response was not at all what he had expected.

'You do what you have to do,' Decker bellowed across the fast-flowing water. As he spoke, he holstered the revolver and readied his long gun. 'He knew the risks when he signed up for this, so let's stop pissing about. You can hear that war going on behind me. Without that poxy ferry we're finished, but if we are then so's your *amigo* here. Which'll it be?'

Jacob felt his guts begin to churn. A lethal cocktail

of fear and uncertainty was infusing his body. He well knew that if he heaved the ferry back to the north bank, both he and his friend were dead meat. And yet his frenzied mind could not produce any solution to the problem. With literally no idea what to do, panic began to take hold of him.

Raoul had watched as the lone sentry dropped out of sight. Some men would have rushed off in pursuit, but not this one. He preferred to linger a while and observe. He was aware that *Mister* Exley and the others would be seething with impatience behind him, but that only brought a sardonic smile to his cruel, thin lips. Let the gringos wait on his word. He well knew what they thought of his kind, but out in the wild, hunting fugitives, they needed him. What he did do was use the time to ensure that his own mount was led back to the horse holder.

After a few moments there was movement at the top of the rise and this time two men stealthily came into view. It was time to unleash Exley's gun thugs.

'I've smoked them, Mister Exley,' he hissed back. 'Two of them with long guns, just as the trail dips down to the river.'

Ben Exley smiled with satisfaction. This was going to be easy. Glancing around at his waiting men, he nodded and gestured them forward. They needed no further urging. This was what they got well paid to do. Crawling on all fours and well spaced out, the five detectives closed in.

It was Brett who opened fire first. His Henry

blasted out in a show of defiance, but in his eager-
ness he had jerked the trigger and the bullet went
wide. He was answered by a volley of shots that just
kept coming, as their assailants worked well-oiled
lever actions with practised speed.

'Jesus,' he exclaimed, as a torrent of hot lead
forced him to duck. 'Who've they got over there,
Wild Bill Hickok his self?'

'That ain't likely,' responded Josh with studied
seriousness. 'I heard tell he took a bullet in the head
up north.'

Brett groaned dispairingly, before rolling to one
side and loosing off another shot. Josh also stood his
ground and began to return fire. For a few moments
there was a stand off. The Pinkertons might have
been hardened professionals, but they were not sui-
cidal. It was then that the bank robbers gained a
temporary advantage. Huey Soble finally joined his
cronies on their left flank. His position allowed him
enfilade fire over the nearest detective. Unseen by
his target, he took careful aim at an almost prone
torso with his revolver and fired. Soble was still troubled by the pain from his wound and so the bullet
went slightly wide, but that actually worked out in his
favour.

The projectile slammed into his victim's skull,
snuffing out that man's life in an instant. As the
Pinkerton agent's body lay twitching in the grass, his
comrades gradually realized what had happened and
their fire petered out. It had been some time since
one of their number had been so swiftly dispatched

in a gunfight and it unnerved them. The odds seemed suddenly not so favourable.

Exley bellowed out, 'Nobody told you to stop shooting, God damn it,' but his words fell on deaf ears.

It was Raoul who got the situation back on track. He had deliberately kept clear of the others and so had remained unobserved by the outlaws. Remaining prone, he calmly and deliberately sighted down the barrel of his Sharps carbine. Not for him the rapid firing Winchesters. He preferred the deadly power and long-range accuracy of his single shot breechloader. As he squeezed the second of the double set triggers, there was not the slightest doubt in his mind about the outcome.

The heavy bullet struck Huey Soble straight through his heart and finally finished what US Marshal Torrance had started. As the broken body collapsed to the ground, Raoul rapidly shifted position and then hollered over to his comrades.

'He's gone straight down to the hot place. Now pour it on, boys. There's only the two of them.'

As the Pinkertons renewed their fire, Brett glanced fearfully at his buddy. 'If Decker don't get a move on, he won't have anyone left to share all that gold with!' It was only after he'd uttered it that he realized the implications of his remark.

As the two riders drew ever closer to the south bank of the Arkansas, the noise of the conflict intensified. 'Sounds like someone's having themselves quite a shindig,' Brad remarked drolly.

103

'Could be that big bastard's bitten off more than he can chew this time,' Klee responded gleefully. 'What say we take a closer look see?'

Brad suddenly reined in and as his gaze locked on to the countryside to the north, his expression darkened. Both the river and ferry crossing remained out of sight, but what he could hear told him plenty. 'A gunfight like that could mean the law's involved and I know for a fact there's paper out on the both of us. We don't want to blunder into the middle of it. I say we ground tether all the animals here and move in on foot.'

His diminutive companion grimaced. 'What if some stray Indian happens by and steals them? We still owe cash money on some of what's on those mules. If we lose everything, we'd be in Shit Street then, for sure.'

Brad groaned and shook his head. 'Bitch, bitch, bitch! I tell you what. You watch our backs with that fine rifle you stole and I'll see to business. My pa told me you've got to speculate to accumulate and there might be some pickings for us up ahead.'

Klee regarded him warily. 'There were too many four-dollar words in that for my liking. Why can't you just speak American like everyone else? And besides,' he added huffily, patting the Winchester's stock, 'I didn't steal this. Its owner just up and died, is all!'

With stolen US Army picket pins securing all the animals, the two men cautiously advanced towards the riverbank. A deeper report sounded off across the water and both men paused. They recognized the sound of a Sharps when they heard it and were now close enough to observe Soble as he collapsed to the ground. Glancing meaningfully at each other, they dropped first into a crouch and then soon after onto all fours. They arrived at the crest of the bank just in time to observe Jacob, as he agonized over what to do; strangely, the one-armed man appeared to be threatening a corpse.

Jacob Stuckey had reached the end of his tether. Across the river, his only friend in the world was bound and in mortal danger and there wasn't a damn thing he could do about it. His mind was seething with anxiety and a host of bad memories. It was as though the late war had returned to haunt him. Sweat pored from his face and his only hand began to shake. It was another ill-chosen remark from Russ Decker that finally broke him.

'Act like a man, you lily-livered piece of piss and get that craft back here!'

Wailing like a tortured banshee, Jacob squeezed the trigger and then, dropping the smoking revolver, turned and leaped into the river. Manically, he struck out towards the nearby south bank.

Decker could hardly believe his eyes. Mark Lansing's apparent demise barely registered with him. It was the suddenly unattended ferry that claimed all his attention. Quickly glancing down at his captive, the outlaw recognized that he too was stunned by the turn of events.

'Some people just can't stand the heat,' Decker muttered. 'And now it looks like it's my turn to get wet. Which means, however you look at it, your time is past,' he added darkly. So saying, he aimed his Winchester at the now superfluous prisoner. Just on the point of squeezing the trigger, his peripheral vision unexpectedly registered movement on the crest of the opposite bank. Taken by surprise, he switched his attention to the two men who had seemingly appeared from nowhere.

'Is it always like this here?' he queried with bewildered frustration.

'Pretty much,' Taggart responded quietly, as he followed his captor's stare. He immediately recognized the newcomers and shook his head in amazement at their uncanny timing. It remained to be seen whether their appearance at such a crucial moment was a good or bad thing. He was soon to find out.

Jacob quickly reached the bank and clawed his way out of the water. The possibility of a bullet in the back never even occurred to him. His only thought was to run and run from his troubles. Those, both past and present, had somehow seamlessly merged, so that he was back in Gettysburg again. John Taggart's current predicament simply no longer figured in his tormented soul. So it transpired, that on looking up, he suddenly spotted two strangers wearing the hated Union blue peering down at him. Then it abruptly dawned on his afflicted mind that they weren't strangers at all and that they weren't even clad in blue.

'Well bless my soul,' Klee remarked ominously.

'This Johnny Reb's just taken a swim. Couldn't have been easy with only the one arm. You reckon he needs some more practice, Brad?'

That man nodded encouragingly. He well knew what was about to happen. 'Yeah, I reckon so.'

Almost casually, Klee lowered the barrel of his newly acquired Winchester until it was pointing directly at Jacob's chest and fired. At almost point blank range, the bullet tore into him with enough velocity to tip him away from the banking and back into the river. With blood pumping from his shattered chest, he hit the water with a great splash.

The current took hold of his broken and helpless body and swept it off to the east. Strangely, in the final seconds before he died, a broad smile spread over Jacob Stuckey's abruptly tranquil features. Whether it was because he had finally escaped his troubled past, or because he knew what John Taggart would do to his killer would never be known.

CHAPTER NINE

As a horrified John Taggart watched his friend's life-less body being swept away in the Arkansas River, everything altered. Suddenly his own survival was all that mattered . . . if only because he had a deadly score to settle. Jacob had meant everything to him. But for that fine man, he definitely wouldn't have survived the War Between the States. Their continuing closeness was the main reason that Taggart had established the ferry crossing, because otherwise a one-armed ex-soldier would have found precious little employment in a rapidly changing and uncaring world. And now, after all that they had experienced together, Jacob Stuckey was gone! Killed by a piece of nameless trash.

Even as Russ Decker's scheming mind adjusted to the altered circumstances, Taggart knew what had to be done. Continuing gunfire indicated that the bank robbers were still resisting and so his trying to reach the posse was not yet likely. Although his hands were still bound, the ever-unpredictable river was the only alternative, but he would have to be quick about it. Because now more than ever he was surplus to requirements, a fact that the outlaw boss had already recognized.

As Decker again swung his Winchester over to cover the prisoner, Taggart flung caution to the winds and launched himself at him. Caught unawares, the outlaw desperately attempted to force the muzzle down, but he was just too late. Taggart got his massive right shoulder under his opponent's arms and heaved. As the two men tumbled heavily onto compacted earth, the rifle discharged harmlessly into the heavens.

With the huge man on top, the outcome of the fight should not have been in doubt, but for the fact that Taggart's wrists were still tightly bound and he was completely unarmed. Coming to an instinctive decision, he viciously headbutted the man beneath him and rolled clear. Decker howled with pain, but he was used to taking hard knocks. Even as his eyes swam with tears, he rapidly worked the lever-action and then struggled to his feet. He was just in time to see his assailant plunge head first into the river. Despite the dangers of that action, it did not escape his notice that such an occurrence was becoming all too commonplace!

As Taggart pitched into the chill depths, he knew that he had to remain submerged and put as much distance between himself and the crossing as possible. Even with his hands tied, that proved remarkably easy with the strong current behind him. It was only when his head began to pound from lack of oxygen that he allowed his powerful legs to take him to the surface. As his head bobbed above the water, he twisted around and peered back upriver. Thankfully, he was already out of effective rifle range and in any case his former captor wasn't even looking his way. It occurred to him that the poxy outlaw quite probably had other things on his mind!

Drawing in deep draughts of air, the ferryman kicked out strongly towards the south bank. It was on that side of the river that Jacob had met his end and where retribution was likely to be meted out. Abruptly, his feet hit solid ground and the current relinquished its dominating hold on him. Remaining in the water and therefore mostly out of sight, he searched for a sharp rock. Once he had one, he acquired a sure footing and began to saw through the rope that secured his wrists. Throughout the whole of that repetitive process, all Taggart could see in his mind's eye was Jacob's bleeding corpse as it plunged helplessly into the Arkansas's depths.

Russ Decker kept his Winchester at the ready, but with the muzzle conspicuously clear of the two new arrivals. He had no idea who or what they were, but one thing was abundantly clear . . . they sure as hell weren't badged up. It was then that he commenced a loud verbal exchange with the larger of the two men both of whom he could well have done without.

'Howdy, friend,' he yelled with forced amiability. 'You can probably tell from the gunplay back here that I would welcome that ferry on this side of the river.'

The other man nodded, but his bearded features were unreadable under the wide brim of his hat. 'I could see how you might think that. You outlawed up or just plain unlucky?'

'Unlucky in my choice of enemies, I guess. I reckon those fellas behind me are either Pinkertons or federal law. Either way, time is short. Which is why I've agreed with myself to make it worth your while.'

Brad spat a stream of evil looking black liquid into the river. His teeth were irreparably stained by tobacco juice. 'Oh, you'll be doing that all right and then some,' he called back. 'The dollar ferry ride disappeared forever with that one-armed son of a bitch. We're the new operators and we take a percentage of everything carried. And I mean everything!'

Beneath his apparently calm demeanour, Decker was seething with anger and frustration. Behind him there had been a short silence followed by a flurry of shots. Sensing that time was running out, he briefly contemplated gunning the two 'land pirates' down, but that was fraught with risk. He had heard the deep report of the smaller man's rifle and recognized that he was probably outgunned. If one of them should survive, he would be effectively marooned and at the mercy of the posse. Bitterly, he accepted that he would have to bite the bullet.

'I guess I'll just have to work with you on that,' he very reluctantly replied.

'I kind of thought you would,' Brad responded in

his deadpan fashion. 'So here's what's gonna happen. My amigo with the buffalo gun will stand watch while I heave the ferry over. Anything you do that he doesn't like, any little thing at all and you're a dead man. Savvy?'

Decker stared at him intently, all the while gnawing on his bottom lip.

'Say it!' Brad barked. 'Or we just sit here and enjoy the show.'

The bank robber coloured. He wasn't used to taking such treatment and it took much self-discipline to respond in an even tone. 'I understand.'

'Good for you, mister,' was Brad's deceptively cheery response. With that, he unbuckled his gun belt and handed it over to Klee. Rapidly descending the slope, he added loudly, 'If I was you, I'd get my possibles together. I ain't hanging around over there for long, on account of that posse might just have paper on us as well.'

Decker lingered for a moment more, watching while the bearded son of a bitch seized the massive cable and entered the water. Then he turned and raced over to the cabin. Suddenly, the only thing on his mind was how to preserve *his* glorious hoard of Gold Double Eagles!

Brett and Josh exchanged desperate glances. Both knew that they couldn't hold out much longer. Empty brass cartridge cases fairly littered the ground and their faces were smudged with black powder residue. Sustained rapid firing meant they were running low on ammunition and now the Pinkertons were extending the semi-circle around them, so as to increase the pressure. The gunfight had been so intense that neither of them had even heard the occasional gunshot from the far side of the river. Even wearing leather gloves, Brett struggled to hold the burning hot barrel of his Henry rifle, as he frantically searched for a target.

It wasn't the first time that he had regretted not obtaining the more modern Winchester, with its protective wooden forestock. Unluckily for the increasingly agitated man, it was another feature of the early repeater that was about to get him killed. Spotting movement, he squeezed the trigger, only to be rewarded with a metallic click. Cursing, he reached into his jacket pocket for the few remaining cartridges.

'Reloading,' he called over to Josh.

Winchesters possessed a side-loading gate, whereas its forerunner had to be reloaded from the muzzle end. That was not always an easy operation for a prone shooter. As Brett rose up from the grass slightly, to slide the spring's tab along the full length of the tubular magazine, another well-aimed bullet from Raoul's Sharps tore into his throat. The outlaw went momentarily rigid with shock and then began to choke on his own blood. No longer in control of his dying body, he briefly stared at his own weapon in apparent amazement, before collapsing to the ground.

Recognizing the sound of the damned Sharps, Josh returned fire, but of course its owner had already wisely shifted position. Anxiously, he then glanced over at the fresh cadaver. 'Are you just wounded or what, Brett?' And then after a tortuous few seconds, 'For Christ's sake, answer me!'

As it dawned on him that he was all that remained of the rearguard, the colour drained from Josh's grubby features. The fact that all shooting had ceased, only seemed to emphasize his sudden isolation.

'Looks like you're all on your lonesome, fella,' taunted a triumphant Ben Exley. 'How's about you throw down your shooting irons and step out into the open? That way you'll live to see another sunrise . . . even if it is through the bars of a jail cell. Ha, ha!'

Josh noisily exhaled through his nose like a horse. 'The hell with this,' he muttered bitterly and then far louder, 'The hell with you, mister!' With that, he discharged one last bullet in the general direction of his tormenter and then scurried back down the slope for the final time. He had no inkling that his last defiant gesture had actually got a result of sorts.

Exley stared in stunned disbelief at the bloody stump where his right forefinger had been. Their lone opponent's last wild shot would have struck him full on in the chest, had he not been holding his rifle slant ways in front of him. As it was, the now badly scored weapon had deflected Josh's bullet, but not before it completely severed the detective's digit. Momentarily overwhelmed by a wave of pain and nausea, Exley groaned and curled over in a foetal position. He was still like that when Raoul crawled over to examine him.

114

'Looks like you'll have to be a left-handed gun from now on, Mister Exley,' the tracker remarked with a complete lack of compassion.

His leader stared up into the cold, hooded eyes and experienced a surge of raw anger, but even though in great distress the Pinkerton man realized that it was more sensible to direct such emotion elsewhere. 'I want that bastard dead, d'you hear me? I want him dead!'

Raoul held the other man's impassioned stare for a moment longer, before offering a rare smile. 'I reckon I can do that,' he responded and then turned away without another word. It was left to one of the other agents to produce a kerchief with which to help stem the flow of blood.

Deputy United States Marshal Sam Torrance was in a bad way, but not so bad that he didn't realise he'd picked up a tail. Not having actually seen anyone, it was more of a feeling really, but he'd been pursuing fugitives far too long to disregard it. And given the elusive nature of his mysterious shadow, it was all too likely to be an Indian.

As another wave of pain lanced through his skull, the lawman knew that he somehow had to exhibit his capacity to resist . . . otherwise he was buzzard bait for sure. Cautiously, he reached up to adjust the makeshift bandage that he had fashioned out of one of his shirtsleeves. He knew without looking that the material was damp with blood, but it would have to suffice, at least until he reached what passed for civilisation out in the mid-west.

With a conscious effort, Torrance used the same hand to shield his eyes temporarily while he searched the surrounding terrain. Up ahead there was a small stand of oak trees and he grunted with satisfaction. Urging his mount forward, he was soon in amongst them. Taking great care that none of the overhanging branches came anywhere near his extremely sensitive skull, the marshal peered around until he saw what he needed.

Struggling against the throbbing agony generated by any form of exertion, he used the hammer that Jonas Bills had generously left him to smash off a thin, straight branch of approximately three feet in length. Then, using his small pocket-knife, he whittled off all the twigs, until his new possession was relatively smooth. The effort required for all this had caused his limbs to tremble. Although it was a far from convincing effort, it would have to do!

Resting the 'butt' of his new 'rifle' on his right thigh, the lawman carefully wheeled his horse around and headed off a short distance down their back trail. Reining in, he conspicuously began to draw a bead on an imaginary enemy in a number of directions, as though demonstrating his complete lack of fear of whoever might be out there. Finally, having made his point and feeling thoroughly worn out, Torrance returned to his original north-westerly course. He knew that he was running a gigantic bluff, which all depended on his secretive companion keeping his distance for a while longer. With the hot sun burning down on him he sighed deeply. The only thing keeping him going was the thought that one day he would catch up with that little pus weasel Bills and beat him flatter than hammered shit!

Josh pounded towards Taggart's cabin as though the hounds of hell were after him. He had no idea how far behind him the posse was, but with every step he expected to hear the sound of that terrifyingly proficient Sharps. Then movement on the river caught his eye and what he witnessed shocked him to his core. The vitally important ferry had finally crossed over, but now appeared to be heading back again. It was already a couple of yards from the landing stage. On board were Russ Decker, two heavily laden horses and some bearded cuss that Josh had never even clapped eyes on before. It was that man who heaved on the cable, whilst the outlaw leader controlled the nervous animals.

'Hey, wait for me,' Josh yelled out in utter desperation.

Taken by surprise, his boss glanced sharply over at him and then said something to his mysterious buddy. That individual merely shook his head and kept on pulling.

Noticeably angry at the curt dismissal, Decker bellowed back at his sole surviving gang member. 'Take a run at it. I'll help you.'

Josh took a fleeting look behind him. There was movement on the crest of the rise. His only chance was the river. Spurred on by sheer terror, he raced towards the wooden decking. With his heart thumping and lungs burning, he rapidly drew closer. Even as his boots hit the timber, he recognized that the ferry was definitely out of reach. Yet if he could just get near and grab the cable, then maybe his boss would pull him in.

'Jump for it,' Decker hollered encouragingly. Under the fraught circumstances, Josh couldn't possibly have realized that Decker's obvious desire for his survival stemmed from more than just genuine fellowship. His boss had seen the very urgent need for back-up when negotiating terms with his two 'rescuers'.

There before him was the glistening water. He had done it. With a last tremendous burst of speed, Josh launched himself across the relentlessly expanding gap. Even as he did so, he hurled his Winchester onto the deck of the ferry. One less thing to worry about. The bullet from Raoul's Sharps struck him when he was literally in mid-air. The stunning shock was quite unbelievable and very suddenly *nothing* was possible anymore. Hitting the surface right next to the cable, he knew he should grab a hold but no longer had any control over his own body. As fresh blood tinged the water, Decker could only watch in dismay as the strong current swept his last man irrevocably out of reach and away to an unknown resting place.

CHAPTER TEN

Raoul had accumulated three kills on this job alone. He had done his bit and in any case, he had spotted the lone figure over on the south bank. The half-breed knew all too well what that meant: covering fire. Veering off to his left, the tracker slipped into the empty cabin and sought out the stove. It was while waiting for the coffee to heat up that he took a look around the chaotic interior. What he saw made his heart pump like an anvil strike. Dollar bills of all denominations were strewn over the floor near one of the cots. The remaining thieves had obviously left in a desperate hurry.

What really popped his cork was the sight of a size-able pile of twenty-dollar bills. His lean face momentarily lit up. Doubtless the money was from the Wichita bank robbery, which meant that he could safely pocket it and no one would be any the wiser. Swiftly, he did just that. To a man like him it was a not-so-small fortune that could change his life – so long as it wasn't discovered on his person. Things were definitely looking up!

Ben Exley was white-faced, but determined. The way to the river was finally clear and he intended to be there when the loot was recovered. Cradling his injured hand, he got shakily to his feet. With his remaining four agents around him, he clambered down the rise just in time to witness a strange thing. The ferry, with two men and horses on its deck, was moving out into the river and yet his tracker was just disappearing into the cabin.

Baffled, the Pinkerton cried out, 'What the hell is the 'breed doing? You men get over to the riverbank and lay down some fire on that God damned ferry.'

With Raoul out of the way, the others were eager to show some colour and so ran forward purposefully. The rapid rifle fire from the far side caught them completely by surprise. It was both accurate and lethal. One man died instantly; the top of his head lifted clean off. Another took a bullet in his right shoulder as he turned to flee and suddenly it was a rout. The three survivors raced or staggered for the cover of the cabin, rejoining their boss on the way. As they reached it, the door abruptly opened.

'Surprised you didn't see that coming,' Raoul remarked matter of factly as they all piled in. 'That long gun over there has got some real power behind it. You can feel it even in here.'

'You could have warned us,' Exley responded bitterly.

The tracker's eyes glinted dangerously. 'The man that made you bleed is feeding the fishes. I figured that had at least earned me a coffee. Besides, even a blind man on a galloping horse could have spotted the rifleman over yonder.'

Exley stared at him wide-eyed for a moment. Not for the first time, Raoul had caught him off balance and this was no time to attempt a rebuke. His wounded agent was bleeding profusely and in great pain *and* with every passing minute the proceeds of the bank robbery were moving further out of reach.

'Fair enough,' he responded evenly. 'But when you've finished your drink, you might see to Tucker before he bleeds to death.' With that, the Pinkerton boss turned away, annoyed with himself. He knew that he was being unfair. Raoul was one of the best in the business, but there was something about the half-breed's manner that got under his skin. Feeling unpleasantly light-headed, he glanced through the cabin's only window and watched the progress of the ferry with frustration. Just what was he going to do about that?

As John Taggart clawed his way up the muddy bank, he heard a gunshot from near the cabin. Knowing that anything that ended up in the water would have to come past him, he decided it was worth investigating and so quickly retraced his steps. As luck would have it, the ferryman spotted the body immediately. It was one of Decker's gun thugs and the Arkansas's treacherous current had conveniently carried the body over towards the south bank.

Steeling himself for another ducking, Taggart plunged into the river and struck out to intercept the luckless outlaw. Just on the point of colliding with the sodden corpse, he turned aside and grabbed hold at the most secure point . . . the gunbelt. Moments later, he heaved Josh's carcass onto relatively dry land. Paying it scant respect, the big man unbuckled the belt, checked the pockets for coins and spare cartridges and then unceremoniously pitched him back into the water. With the comforting feel of a weapon now strapped to his waist, Taggart glared back upriver. In addition to avenging his friend, he also wanted his God damned crossing back!

Russ Decker was absolutely mortified. The ferry had come to a stop in almost exactly the same place as it had been when the one armed cockchafer had originally escaped on it. The new 'operator' stood with his hand resting lightly on the thick cable. Already Brad had adopted a proprietorial manner, as though genuinely considering that the river crossing and everything connected to it now belonged to him. A superior smile briefly flitted across his bearded features and then he got down to business.

'Those fellas in the cabin suddenly don't seem keen to interfere. Klee often has that affect on people, so I reckon this is as good a place as any to talk business. Oh and in case you're tempted to use that carbine, you might recollect just how handy my partner is with his new toy. He might not look much, but he's one mean son of a bitch.'

Decker glanced over at the diminutive figure standing on the south bank and sighed. It was quite obviously a Winchester in his hands, but it appeared somehow more robust and powerful than the models that he was familiar with. And there was no doubting his ability with it.

'So how much do you *need* to set me down on dry land?' he queried, doing his best to hide the anger that surged through him. He was acutely aware that he was now an outlaw leader without a gang.

Brad guffawed jovially, but any humour completely failed to reach his hard eyes. 'Now that kind of depends on what you're carrying in those saddle bags. Open one of them up, so's I can take a peek,' he instructed.

Decker gripped his long gun so hard that his knuckles turned white. Momentarily he considered driving the horses forward, into and over the bearded bastard and then taking his chances in the water, but then common sense returned. Slowly and very reluctantly he began to unbuckle the nearest bag.

Maybe it had been the river water or more likely Naylor's old needle, but one way or another the wound had become infected. The constant pain emanating from his ear gnawed at Teach like a cancer, and Baxter's irritating presence served as a continuous reminder of just whose fault it was. Since fleeing Dodge City, that man had very sensibly kept his distance and held his tongue, but their companions knew that it was only a matter of time before he slipped up.

123

The previous night, the keelboat had briefly pulled in to the north bank of the Arkansas River just outside the city of Great Bend, Kansas. The former cow town was considerably more peaceful than Dodge and Naylor had been able to sneak in and steal some food without provoking a hue and cry. After that, the craft and its reluctant crew had followed the river around the 'great bend' from which the settlement had been named. From then on they would be heading relentlessly southeast into the Indian Territories, coincidentally passing close to the city of Wichita.

It was frustration at his lack of cash and genuine concern over their eventual destination that ultimately led Barf Baxter into a world of hurt. The sound of persistent gunfire downriver had him reaching for one of the sturdy wooden poles and he didn't even bother to ask permission from his supposed leader. Jabbing it into the river bottom, he began to alter the course of the shallow-drafted craft.

Despite his deteriorating condition, Ed Teach had insisted on remaining as helmsman and now regarded Baxter with irrational fury.

'Get that God damn pole back in the boat,' he snarled, showering spittle over the deck. 'I say where we go!'

'There's shooting up ahead,' Baxter retorted angrily. 'You've no idea where you're taking us anyway and I sure as hell ain't going to take a bullet for you.'

Teach's sickly pallor abruptly disappeared as his hairy features took on a scarlet hue. 'You gutless piece of shit,' he barked out. 'I've taken all I'm going to from you. It's time to come to conclusions.' With that, he simply released his grip on the steering oar and barrelled down the starboard side of the boat.

Not for the first time, Rio cried out, 'Oh, not again!' Yet this time he wasn't able to step in and take over immediately. He was well to the front of the craft and had all his efforts on keeping his footing as it veered sharply to the right. And then he too heard the shooting down river. 'Perhaps we should pull in to the bank, boss,' he called. 'Just until we find out what's happening up ahead.'

He might as well have been talking to the man in the moon, because their crazed leader continued on his manic course. This time Baxter had nowhere to run to and like so many he had never learned to swim. As he stared aghast at Teach's massive figure advancing on him, any semblance of logical thought left him. Instead of drawing a weapon, he dragged his ten-foot long pole from the water and swung it around in a great sweeping blow.

If it had connected, it would have sent his assailant flying, but Teach merely ducked under it and with a triumphant roar launched himself across the last few feet. Belatedly realizing his mistake, Baxter dropped the pole as though it was made from hot coals, but before he could draw his knife the big man was upon him.

Days of pent up anger and frustration resulted in Teach resorting to the most primeval form of assault. Reaching out, he seized his unfortunate victim by the throat with devastating force. 'I'm gonna crush you like a bug,' he informed him through gritted teeth.

'For Christ's sake, boss, you'll kill him,' Naylor cried out in protest, but he made no attempt to intervene.

Rio might have stepped in, but his prime concern was to save the boat. It was heading straight for the south bank and certain destruction. Just as on the last occasion when he had saved them, he grabbed the steering oar and heaved it over with all his might.

Oblivious to anything other than his constricting airway, Baxter kicked and punched with all his failing strength, but it was to no avail. The great brute had him in a death grip that could have only one outcome. Spittle showered over his face as his assailant cried out in triumph. As the dying man's vision began to cloud, he instinctively seized his knife and plunged its keen blade into Teach's side. It proved to be his last action on God's earth. The huge man howled like the wounded beast that he was, but rather than relinquish his hold he instead pushed Baxter over to the forward gunwale. Then, uttering a great roar, he literally lifted his victim off the deck and hurled him over the side.

Rio had just regained control of the keelboat when two things claimed his attention in quick succession. Necessarily ignoring the desperate struggle in the bow, he peered ahead and suddenly noticed, a short distance downriver, another craft. Only this one appeared to be stationary. With other matters on his mind, it took him a few moments to recognize it for what it was: a ferry connected to both banks by a stout cable. Reacting with a landlubber's mentality, the realization that the Arkansas was effectively blocked horrified him. With no idea what to do, panic began to surge through his body. Then, as if that wasn't bad enough, he witnessed Baxter's corpse hurled over the side and instinctively jerked the steering oar to avoid him.

Up in the front of the boat, Naylor witnessed Baxter's demise with dismay. Superstitiously crossing himself, he whispered, 'Adios, compadre. At least you finally took a bath!'

Teach collapsed to his knees, clutching his side. The dead man's blade remained in his flesh and he was undecided as to how to stem the flow of blood. Whether it was a mortal wound was not immediately apparentt to Naylor, but the scene held his fascinated attention until, to his great surprise he heard raised voices directly in front of them. Glancing downriver, he was absolutely appalled to see a ferry complete with passengers only yards away. One of the men on board was actually pointing a weapon at him, so he dropped down below the gunwale and helplessly waited for the impact.

Sam Torrance had completely lost track of time. The throbbing in his head just never went away and all the time he had to keep checking the horizon for any sign of whoever was trailing him. The sound of gunfire off to the northeast had come as a complete surprise to him, but in a way it was a relief. It meant that there were at least some tangible people up ahead, rather than the mysterious, unseen phantom that he was still convinced was on his tail. Or just maybe he was so far gone that his mind was playing tricks on him.

Wearily, the lawman reined in and glanced up at the sun. Then he spent a while scrutinizing his surroundings. Despite the constant pain, it suddenly came to him that he was back on vaguely familiar territory, which could only mean that John Taggart and his friend appeared to be in some kind of trouble. He had been hoping to get help at the crossing, but it now seemed as though it was the massive ferryman who was in need as well. Torrance shook his head in resignation and instantly regretted it. Then, clutching his homemade rifle, he urged his tired animal forward. He had always prided himself on the fact that he could handle any situation that came his way and now that belief was about to be put to the test!

Brad's eyes widened like saucers as they settled on the gleaming gold coins in the saddle-bag. He'd never seen so much of anything worth having in one place before. No wonder the son of a bitch next to him was so desperate to get across the river.

'What is it? What's he carrying?' came a call from the riverbank. There was no hiding the eager curiosity in Klee's voice.

Brad's mind was suddenly a mass of competing ideas. How could he relieve this stranger of the gold without sharing it with his diminutive companion?

Under the strained circumstances, it was remarkable that anyone actually spotted the new arrival on the river, but a flicker of movement somehow registered in

Klee's peripheral vision. Twitching with surprise, he glanced to his left and suddenly all his attention was taken by the long, sleek craft heading directly towards the ferry.

'Sweet Jesus! What are they up to?' he cried out. His concern was genuine, but related more to whatever was in the saddle-bags than to the survival of the men before him. 'Move your ass, Brad,' he bellowed out. 'They're out to ram you for sure!'

Otherwise occupied, that man glanced around utterly bewildered. Then both he and Decker saw the keelboat and the colour drained from their faces. Temporarily unarmed, Brad could only stare in horror at the vessel slicing through the water towards them. His passenger had a greater range of options. Decker fired one warning shot before desperately searching for a live target. Somehow sensing danger, the horses beside him snickered nervously.

Two men appeared to be sheltering behind the forward gunwale, whilst a third man was at the rear, but he was mostly protected by the central cabin. Cursing vividly, the bank robber got one more shot off, before reluctantly accepting that they were going to be rammed. A louder report sounded on the riverbank, but completely failed to alter the inevitable.

It was then that Russ Decker proved just how resourceful he really was. Hurling his Winchester over to the south bank, he hissed at Brad, 'You'd better swim for it, fella.'

Brad glanced at him in dismay. 'I never learned.'

'Shouldn't be running a ferry then,' Decker

muttered as he grabbed the saddle-bags off his animal. The keelboat was nearly upon them and timing would be critical.

With the collision mere seconds away, he heard a loud splash and grinned mirthlessly. The new ferry operator had obviously overcome his fear of water and abandoned ship, his career effectively over. Gripping the heavy bags in both hands, Decker swung them around in a full circle and then with a tremendous heave sent them on their way ... directly into the approaching craft!

With a great rending crash, the inevitable impact occurred. At that very moment he sucked in a deep breath and leapt into the river on the opposite side to Brad and Klee. No one could have foreseen the unlikely outcome of the collision. Drawing such a shallow draft, the keelboat literally rode up over the strongly constructed ferry, bowling Decker's horses aside as though they were mere skittles. Wrenched from their tethers, the poor creatures screamed in anguish as they plunged into the river, to be swept away like so many men had been that day.

The inertia created by the sheer weight of the silver ore prevented the boat from simply slipping on into the water. Instead it ground to a halt on top of the ferry, which in turn settled just below the surface, still connected to both banks by its thick cable. The fact that that lifeline still remained in place was a bonus for Russ Decker. Clinging to it like a limpet, he stared in amazement at the now conjoined craft and pondered how to recover his 'Double Eagles'.

CHAPTER ELEVEN

Ben Exley couldn't believe his eyes. Even the throbbing agony in his right hand was temporarily expunged by the extraordinary events on the Arkansas River. Any sane man would have expected to see the whole 'kit and kaboodle' drifting off with the current and yet the remaining outlaw and his ill-gotten gains appeared to be still within reach . . . just!

Glancing around at his surviving agents, he quickly deliberated over which one to send in pursuit. His choice was really very simple, but he hated having to rely on the same man yet again. Sighing, he turned away from the window. One thing was for sure, there was paper money aplenty strewn around the cabin, but no gold.

'Raoul, I've got a big ask for you.'

That man's reptilian eyes bored into his for a long moment, before he demonstrated yet again that very little escaped his notice. 'If I go into that river, Mister Exley, I ain't just on wages anymore.'

The Pinkerton boss recoiled slightly. He had

noticed before that once away from civilization the half-breed tracker became kind of uppity, until sometimes Exley wondered just who was in charge. It had to stop and so, although time was short and the situation desperate, he decided he wasn't prepared to roll over entirely.

'*If* you recover some of the bank's funds, I guarantee you a cash bonus. And if that means swimming the Arkansas, then so be it. Truth is, if it wasn't for this hand, I'd do it myself.'

As he regarded the dapper agent in his bowler and smart duds, spoilt only by copious bloodstains, Raoul smiled bleakly. He had always considered his boss to be a blowhard city slicker, out of his depth on the frontier and so consequently it wasn't quite a done deal. 'And anything Wells Fargo lays claim to counts as well,' he added pointedly.

Exley gritted his teeth. The raw stump where his trigger finger had been was paining him something awful. 'Yeah, yeah. Of course,' he snapped. 'Just get moving.'

Raoul deliberately held his gaze for a moment longer. He *still* wasn't finished. 'Answer me this. Why don't we just shoot everything that moves on that boat and then recover the money in our own sweet time?'

Exley's eyes widened in genuine horror. 'Because we don't know who all's on it, that's why. We're paid to enforce the law and those rivermen could simply be honest traders who lost control of it. We can't just kill everyone that we come across. And when you get over there, you'll remember that. Clear?'

Raoul favoured him with a thin smile, before bending down to remove his footwear. 'I guess so, but I sure ain't risking a pair of ten dollar boots in that river,' he declared by way of explanation. Turning away, he stowed them under one of the two cots and in doing so slipped his thick wad of twenty-dollar bills tightly inside one of the finely crafted leather boots.

'You two fellas keep me covered, you hear?' he growled at the remaining able-bodied agents as he made for the door. 'This ain't the day I die in some river!'

Mere seconds before the collision, Naylor got the shock of his worthless life. Seemingly from out of nowhere, two heavy saddle-bags tumbled into view and thumped down on the deck next to him. But that was far from all. One of the pouches hadn't been fastened properly and as it flew through the air, gold coins suddenly cascaded over him. The outlaw's jaw literally dropped in amazement and his tongue flopped moronically into view, as though he intended to taste his unexpected windfall.

Then one craft hit the other with a shocking impact that jarred Naylor's teeth together. The trauma of biting through his own tongue drained all the colour from his face and temporarily blotted out any thoughts of the gold. The bow of the keelboat then rode up over the ferry, sending the two horses on it careering into the water. Naylor, whose mouth was now foaming with blood, helplessly rolled backwards. All the while there was a tremendous creaking and groaning sound, as though the timbers beneath him were actually alive and suffering.

Ed Teach was also bleeding profusely from the wound in his side, but his eyes lit up with glee at the sight of the glorious 'Double Eagles'. Even the great impact failed to deflect his rapt attention. Every man and his dog knew that gold was worth far more than the stinking silver ore that they had saddled themselves with. What happened next, however, did give him something else to think on.

The soaking wet figure of Russ Decker suddenly vaulted over the gunwale. In his right hand he clutched a cocked revolver. 'I don't know who you stupid sons of bitches are, but those saddle bags belong to me, so back off!'

Naylor, still addled by pain and shock, mumbled something unintelligible. Flecks of his blood landed on some of the coins, which found little favour with Decker.

'I said back off, you dumb bastard.' He stared at him curiously. 'What ails you, anyhow?'

'Mu, mu,' was Naylor's pathetic attempt at conversation, but it did serve to claim Decker's momentary interest.

Ed Teach, having already decided that the gold was now his, took the opportunity to draw his revolver, but blood loss and pain slowed him down. Even as he cleared leather, the movement registered on Decker's peripheral vision. The bank robber turned to his left and dropped the hammer. To his great relief, the cartridge had remained watertight and detonated with a satisfying crash.

The heavy bullet struck Teach in his chest. Already weakened by the knife thrust, he stared down in stunned amazement as blood seeped out of the latest hole in his body.

'Everything's against me today,' he muttered plaintively, before falling face down onto the deck. As luck would have it, he died with a gold 'Double Eagle' pressing firmly into his grubby forehead.

It was gunfire on or near the river that alerted him to a changing situation. As John Taggart stealthily made his way back along the bank, he was utterly appalled at the sight of a rogue poleboat heading straight for his ferry. He only just stifled a warning cry. Jacob's diminutive killer was standing guard further down the bank, his attention fully occupied by the events on the river and Taggart wanted to keep it that way. Besides, those on the ferry were no friends of his. He flinched as the inevitable collision occurred, but maintained his silence. The ferry could be rebuilt, but he would have to be alive to do it.

It was said that nobody knew how to hate like an Indian, but as the massive ferryman moved in on his prey, his heart was filled with venom. The man before him had murdered his only true friend and now he would pay. A single shot rang out on the keelboat and Klee took aim, but held his fire. He was obviously not directly threatened and choosing to wait on events.

'Well he won't have to wait much longer,' Taggart

decided. Staying low, so as to remain hidden from those on the river, he moved around in a wide arc that kept him behind the little bastard. Josh's Colt was cocked and ready in its new owner's hand. Taking it in a two-handed grip, that man aimed directly at Klee's back. His finger was just tightening on the trigger when a bearded face unexpectedly appeared over the brow of the banking. Even though sodden and bedraggled, it was still immediately recognizable.

Brad's eyes betrayed his sudden shock at the scene before him and provided his partner with a warning of sorts. Klee, his reactions honed from years on the dodge, twisted around to face his assailant with the speed of a cat, but even that wasn't fast enough. Taggart's bullet tore into his right shoulder. The agony that coursed through his right arm caused the scrawny cuss to drop his heavy rifle. Taggart, noting that Brad appeared to be unarmed, concentrated all his fury on Jacob's killer.

'You've got this coming, you little runt,' he snarled. Cocking and firing in one fluid motion, he deliberately placed another piece of lead straight into Klee's other shoulder. 'That was for Jacob and all the other poor southern boys you've harmed!' The little man's eyes bulged in their sockets as he tried to comprehend what was happening to him, but the pain surging through his tortured body was overwhelming. As he tottered feebly backwards, his persecutor added, 'And this is for me.'

The third bullet struck Klee's skull. The little man

died messily, but without a sound, his shattered body toppling backwards into the Arkansas River. As luck would have it, he entered the water in exactly the same place as his one-armed victim had earlier that day. Although nodding with satisfaction, John Taggart felt a strange emptiness come over him. He might have avenged his friend, but nothing was going to bring him back again. And yet he was to be allowed little time for reflection.

Taking advantage of Taggart's pre-occupation, Brad charged towards him and kicked his feet out from under. The massive ferryman went down like a felled oak, dropping his revolver in the process, but the outlaw had sense enough to recognize that he was unlikely to come out on top in a fistfight. Playing safe, he went for the rifle that he had coveted so much after the grisly death of Jonas Bills. As his hands closed around the heavy weapon, he turned to finish the job . . . and found his opponent not only back on his feet, but coming straight for him.

Instinctively, Brad knew that he wouldn't be able to level the rifle in time, so instead he swung it around at head height. Unfortunately for him, his enemy was taller even than Abe Lincoln had been and so the stock merely slammed into a solid shoulder. Taggart grunted with pain and recoiled slightly. He was still struggling to recover the wind that had been knocked out of him. Brad kept on coming and unleashed another swing. On this occasion, the big man managed to block it and at the same time grab hold of the barrel. Brad was no lightweight himself and he had enough power and momentum behind him to force Taggart back to the ground. Desperately the two men struggled in the grass for possession of the Winchester.

'I should have killed you days ago when I had the chance,' the ferryman spat out.

'What the hell's happening over there?' Ben Exley had been watching Raoul as that man dragged his way across the fast flowing river, but was now distracted by the outbreak of violence on the far bank. One thing was for sure; he and his men would no longer be under threat from that quarter. 'You two, get back out there,' he commanded. 'Cover Raoul, but no shooting unless I say so. With luck they'll all kill each other, without us having to do anything.'

Leaving their badly wounded associate to bleed out, the three men moved outside and over towards the landing stage. It was then that the Pinkerton boss suddenly glimpsed an unknown horseman heading towards the south bank.

'Who *are* all these people?' he muttered.

Russ Decker heard the report of a revolver up on the nearest riverbank and instinctively ducked down behind the gunwale. Two more shots crashed out and then he glimpsed a body tumble down the banking and into the water.

'There sure is some blood-letting going on around here today,' he remarked, only half to himself. Turning his attention back to the stranded boat, he was just in time to see the man with the bleeding mouth disappear around the side of the central cabin. His temporary isolation only seemed to highlight his own particular problem. He was still in possession of the stolen gold, but he had nowhere to go with it. The God damn boat was almost high and dry. Pinkertons controlled the north bank and whoever was left to the south would doubtless want to steal it from him.

Sighing, the bank robber quickly collected up the fallen coins and secured them in the saddle-bag. Then, with the germ of an idea forming, he decided to see just who else there was on the boat. Making his way cautiously towards the rear, he went along the other side to that taken by Naylor, so as to keep the bulk of the cabin between himself and the remaining Pinkertons.

That man was unsuccessfully trying to describe the presence of some glorious gold coins to his only remaining companion. Rio had sensibly kept to the back of the boat during and after the collision. He hadn't realized that the shot that killed Teach had actually been triggered on board. Now he was trying to make sense of a man with no tongue and whose features were dripping with blood and snot. Then a big son of a bitch, whom he had never clapped eyes on before, came around the side of the cabin holding a cocked revolver. Belatedly, Rio made a move for his own gun.

'Don't even think about it,' hissed Decker. 'You'd be already dead if I didn't need you for something.

Do what I tell you and I might let both of you live.'

The knife-fighter regarded him curiously, before demonstrating just how sharp he really was. 'If you're by chance wanting this boat back in the water, then you're wasting your time, mister.'

Decker was impressed, but did his best to hide the fact. 'And why might that be?'

'Because when we stole it in Colorado, it was full of silver ore and we haven't yet found anyone fool enough to buy it. All of which means this is one heavy sucker!'

Decker considered that response for a moment, before proving that he too was no dullard. 'This thing's known as a poleboat, yeah? Which means it's got poles on board. Get one apiece and mosey on down to the sharp end. Oh and drop that gunbelt, so's you don't get tempted.' Clicking his fingers, he added, 'And make it snappy. Everybody seems to want a piece of what I'm packing.'

With air back in his lungs, John Taggart began to feel his immense strength returning. Both men still gripped the heavy Winchester. Whoever got control of that would without doubt be the victor. Although his adversary was still on top of him, legs straddling his body, the massive ferryman had the ground beneath him to use for leverage. With a tremendous surge of power, he suddenly extended his arms and twisted the weapon to one side. As Brad began to lose his dominant position, Taggart redoubled his efforts to retain the advantage. Sweat pored from his bearded face, but he just couldn't stop the inevitable. It was like fighting a man mountain.

Taggart grunted with satisfaction as he rolled the other man onto his side. Now all he needed was to yank the rifle from his grasp, but that was easier said than done. Brad clung on with the strength of desperation, before suddenly doing the unexpected. Releasing one hand, he bunched it into a fist and planted a vicious blow onto Taggart's nose. The outlaw was rewarded with the agreeable crunch of breaking bone. His opponent had been in fights before, but nothing could have prepared the ferryman for the shocking pain that spread over his face. Tears unavoidably welled up in his eyes, completely clouding his sight.

Sensing victory, Brad unleashed another brutal clout that only compounded Taggart's misery, before returning his full attention to the rifle. With two hands again holding it, he gave a tremendous heave and abruptly it was back in his possession. What he should really have done then was clamber back out of reach and open fire, but he was consumed by an overwhelming bloodlust. His only desire was to bludgeon his troublesome opponent to death with the gun butt. Drawing his arms back, he lined up a tremendous swing at Taggart's defenceless skull.

The blow, when it landed, struck with the dreadful force of a sledgehammer, shattering bone and unleashing a mess of blood and brain matter. Death was instantaneous and the lifeless body lay slumped on the sun-baked ground, fit only for carrion birds.

John Taggart's vision finally began to clear. The pain in and around his nose was intolerable, but there was also no denying the amazing fact that he was still alive. Screwing his eyes up against the bright light, he gazed up at the strange shape looming over him.

'Never thought I'd see that lovely rifle again,' Sam Torrance muttered, his voice laced with exhaustion, 'Or my horse. This bull turd must have had a run in with my prisoner. I guess that means I won't be seeing Jonas Bills again.' There was a thump, as the US Marshal dropped something heavy and then, very slowly, he sank down onto the grass next to the man whose life he had just saved. 'I've brought your hammer back. Thought you might have missed it!'

CHAPTER TWELVE

As the Pinkerton Detective Agency's tracker labori-
ously heaved his way, arm over arm, across the
Arkansas River, he roundly cursed Ben Exley. Raoul's
water-logged clothes were acting as a drag on him
and he was cold and angry. All his life, he'd had to
eat dirt from the likes of the Pinkerton boss, but it
was going to be different after this job. His stash of
twenty-dollar bills would see to that. Yet for the
present, he still had to finish the job in hand.

He paused for a moment to catch his breath and
check on the situation. Because the ferry was now
mostly under water, the cable that he clung to was
taut and completely submerged. Which in turn
resulted in his being barely visible above the surface
and as yet undiscovered. There had been shooting
up on the crest of the south bank and now there was
nobody in sight, which was possibly a good thing.
Reliance on others did not come easily to Raoul, but
he knew that he would just have to trust Exley and his

men to protect him from any threat over there. Then he witnessed a strange thing.

Two men clutching long poles gingerly lowered themselves over the side of the keelboat, so that they were soon standing with their feet awash on the ferry. Another fellow with a gun appeared to be threatening them. They then wedged their poles under the bow of the boat and began to heave on them. Raoul scoffed at their efforts. With the current flowing against the stern, he reckoned that they had little chance of success.

Decker peered over the side and swore. He had scant knowledge of riverboats, but common sense now told him that the weight of the silver combined with the current meant that his prisoners' efforts were doomed to failure. So, if he couldn't go back, then he might as well go forward. It didn't matter a damn where the craft took him, so long as it was out of reach of the tarnal Pinkertons!

'You're wasting your time with them poles,' Decker hollered. 'You with the big knife. Cut through that cable pronto and you're a free man.'

Rio, up to his ankles in water and thoroughly unhappy, was horrified. 'If I cut through the rope, this whole God damn thing'll go sideways. I might be crushed to death!'

Decker regarded him bleakly. 'Well yeah, I'll allow that *might* happen, but if you don't do it you're a dead man for sure!'

Rio stared up at the muzzle of the revolver pointing directly at him and briefly weighed his options.

Naylor, blood-soaked and miserable, had immediately ceased work and was just staring numbly at the encroaching water. He would be no help at all in any standoff. It seemed that the reluctant river pirate had no choice.

Drawing his broad-bladed Bowie Knife, Rio moved over to the edge of the submerged ferry nearest the south bank. Once the cable was cut, he would then with luck be able to use the remains of it to get to dry land. If he didn't get shot in the back first! Shaking his head with distaste, he crouched down and slipped into the water. Gripping the massive rope with his left hand, he began to cut into the strands.

Raoul watched as the man drew his knife and reluctantly entered the river. He knew exactly what that signified and couldn't let it stand. Drawing his own knife, he wedged it between his teeth and then rapidly began closing on the conjoined craft. His almost submerged approach remained unseen by the two men left aboard. Naylor was in a world of his own, whilst Decker continued to train his revolver on the man doing the work.

Reaching the north facing side of the ferry, the Pinkerton man took in a deep breath and then launched himself under the solid framework. Gripping the timbers, he pulled his way across until he was able to see the legs of his target. His instinct was to strike a mortal blow, but then Exley's words came back to him. 'We can't just kill everyone that we come across'.

Raoul paused momentarily, before deciding, 'The hell with it. It's my life!'

Kicking out strongly, he aimed directly at his prey's belly, only to be thwarted as Rio abruptly shifted position to get a better grip. Nevertheless, the blade penetrated deep into that man's left thigh. Suddenly assailed by shocking pain, he still had sufficient presence of mind to know exactly what had happened. In his home state, Rio had gained a fearsome reputation as a knife-fighter and so reacted with lightning speed. Relinquishing his hold on the cable, he ducked underwater and swept his blade from side to side. Startled by the sudden defence, Raoul swam to his right, hoping for an opening that he could exploit.

Up in the keelboat, Decker simultaneously spotted both the bloodstains in the water and the would-be assassin. 'Sweet Jesus,' he exclaimed. 'It's just one thing after another!'

Taking rapid aim, he fired down into the river. His hurried shot missed, but it had the effect of bringing a hornet's nest down on him. On the north bank, Exley bellowed out, 'He must be shooting at Raoul. Open fire!'

His two men opened up with their Winchesters, sending a fusillade of hot lead towards the boat. Their firing was enthusiastic rather than accurate, but it had the effect of sending Decker down onto the deck. With that man immobilised, Rio no longer had any reason to remain, but sadly he was now quite unnecessarily fighting for his life. Aided by the water's

146

buoyancy, his wound was not quite the handicap that it would have been on land. With practised skill, the seasoned knife-fighter jabbed his weapon forward, all the time shifting it from hand to hand to confuse his opponent.

Recognizing that he was up against a professional, Raoul remained on the defensive. Their blades clashed, but with his superior mobility he managed to remain just out of reach. The man-hunter well knew that whoever needed air first was finished and that was likely to be his adversary.

With his deep wound bleeding profusely, Rio could feel himself weakening. His head was pounding and he desperately needed air. If only he could make a kill first. Abruptly tucking in both arms before him, he kicked out strongly. The pain in his left leg was sickening, but the move had succeeded in confusing the Pinkerton. Rio couldn't be sure from which angle the next attack would come. All he could do was retreat and he only just made it.

Rio's left hand streaked out. The knife point sliced through Raoul's cotton shirt and carved a shallow wound across his chest. Belatedly, he brought his own blade in to attack, but his assailant suddenly wasn't there. Rio couldn't remain under water any longer and had surfaced just to the south of the vessels. Frantically sucking air into his lungs, he wildly slashed around him but it was a hopeless effort. He just could not cope with any assault from underneath.

Shaken by his narrow escape, Raoul moved in on

his defenceless prey like an attacking shark. Coming from below, his blade viciously lanced up into Rio's groin. That man howled in agony as he thrashed about. The next penetration came in his belly and then it was quite simply all over. Rio relinquished his hold on the big Bowie and surrendered to the Arkansas's current. As yet another bleeding corpse was swept off to the south-east, Raoul gratefully filled his lungs. There was a smile on his face. Yet again he had come out on top. There seemed to be no stopping him.

John Taggart peered cautiously over the crest of the banking. He was just in time to see Raoul's head break the surface. The grinning stranger had a knife in each hand and one of them was a very distinctive Bowie. On the keelboat, Russ Decker had scrambled over to the south side to escape the Pinkertons' persistent gunfire. The massive ferryman had no idea who it was in the river, but he easily recognized the bank robber and so rapidly backed off.

'Mind if I borrow your fine rifle?' he quietly asked the recumbent marshal.

That man stared up at him sternly. 'I reckon. But don't forget that I carry the law. I won't see you murder anyone, you hear?'

Taggart nodded wearily. 'There's been more than enough killing on account of this river crossing.' So saying, he returned to the crest and took aim.

He was just in time, because Decker had decided that he didn't like the look of the lone swimmer. Not that he ever really took to anyone. After checking that the cabin was between him and the Pinkertons, the outlaw swung his revolver over the weathered gunwale.

Without any warning the rifle bullet smacked into timber, sending splinters into the left side of Decker's face. He yelped with pain and surprise and then sensibly froze. Treading water below him, Raoul twisted around as he searched for the latest threat. So it was that when Taggart rose to his full height, he had both their attention.

'You, felon,' he called out. 'You so much as twitch without my say so and you're dead. Savvy?'

Decker stared at him in silent disbelief, before nodding slowly.

'You in the water,' Taggart continued. 'I don't know who you are, so get onto the ferry and keep quiet. And don't even think about using those toothpicks or I'll blow you to hell!' Without waiting for a response, he raised his voice and boomed out across the river. 'You there. Identify yourselves!'

He didn't have long to wait.

'We're employed by the Pinkerton Detective Agency,' replied Ben Exley. 'Charged with recovering all monies stolen from the Farmers' and Merchants' Bank in Wichita. The man in the water works for me.'

Despite the situation, Taggart chuckled. He held an ace in the hole that was going to make the fellows across the river mighty unhappy.

'Well, Mister Pinkerton man, my name's John Taggart. I own this crossing and I've got a federal officer over here who'll vouch for me.' In a muttered aside, he added, 'That's if he ever gets up again.'

'I heard that, you son of a bitch,' retorted the marshal painfully.

'So he'll be taking control of any money recovered,' Taggart continued remorselessly.

There was a stunned silence on the north bank as Exley digested that, but it didn't last long. 'I'll need more than just your word to convince me of that. I've no knowledge of any federal officer working in these parts. I need proof!'

'I'll get to that,' Taggart replied, before putting the Pinkertons firmly from his mind. Glancing over at Decker he instructed, 'Toss that hand gun into the river, now.'

Decker glared back at him and did nothing. The powerful Winchester crashed out again and the bullet missed him by a whisker before slamming into the cabin.

'Don't test me, mister,' the ferryman barked. 'I've got a powerful urge to kill you.'

As the revolver dropped into the water close to Raoul, Taggart glanced down at him. 'You really one of Allan Pinkerton's men?'

The other man nodded eagerly, keen to get back on dry land.

'What's with the bleeding mute over there? Who's he work for?'

'I think he came on the keelboat,' Raoul answered. 'Can I get out of here now? I'm bleeding myself.'

'Uhuh,' Taggart responded with a notable lack of sympathy. 'But I want you on the boat first. There must be a river anchor somewhere in the cabin. Get moving.'

Despite his unfavourable situation, Raoul eyed the big man dangerously. 'Just who do you think you are, talking to me in such a way?'

The ferryman favoured him with a cold smile. 'I'm a man with a big gun and an itch to use it. Don't test me, boy.'

Although seething with anger, Raoul swam over to the ferry and climbed on to its waterlogged decking. From there, he boarded the boat and disappeared into the cabin. Bare moments passed before he returned holding a long coil of rope and dragging a heavy anchor. In all their time on the craft, Teach and his associates hadn't even thought to look for such a thing.

'So what do I do with this, man with a big gun?' he queried.

Completely ignoring the sarcasm, Taggart was quick to respond. 'Wedge it behind the gunwale. That's the side of the boat to you. And then take a short swim over here with the rope.'

Raoul glared at him, but again did as he was instructed. In spite of his instinctive resentment of all authority, he was beginning to develop a grudging admiration for the big man, who seemed to know exactly what he was about.

A short while later, Raoul arrived on the south bank holding the rope end. Taggart was quick to utilize it. There were six animals grazing near the river. Ignoring the heavily laden mules, he picked the two sturdiest horses and fastened the rope around their saddle horns. Glancing down at the marshal, he asked, 'You able to ride one of these?'

That man slowly got to his feet. 'I reckon so.'

The ferryman smiled at him with genuine warmth, before moving back to the crest. 'Decker,' he called out. 'Best gather up those saddle bags and hold tight. You ain't going far, but it'll be bumpy.' Then his eyes settled on Naylor's pathetic figure. 'You'd best get clear, fella,' he hollered.

That man gazed up at him numbly, but made no effort to move.

'Suit yourself,' Taggart grunted, before turning to the dripping tracker. 'Take a pull on this rope with me, huh. That's no lightweight down there.' As the two men took a firm grip, he beckoned at Sam Torrance. 'Anytime you're ready, old man.'

The marshal's likely response was lost in the sound of hoof beats and human grunting as all involved strained on the rope. They in turn were soon overwhelmed by tremendous creaking and rending noises from the Arkansas, as all the effort got a result, albeit not one that Taggart had intended. The keelboat was dragged off the ferry all right, but the iron anchor destroyed the gunwale in the process. With the boat hitting the river side on, it immediately began to take on water.

Decker instantly recognized the danger. He had wisely remained at the front and so quickly heaved his saddle-bags onto the now visible ferry, before following on himself. Naylor, who had been shaken off his feet, gazed in bewilderment at their sudden arrival.

'Don't even think about it,' Decker snarled, although in truth the Double Eagles really weren't his anymore.

Taggart watched as the boat sank below the surface. 'Well that didn't pan out quite the way I intended,' he remarked. 'But at least I've got my ferry back.' The big man chuckled for the first time in two days, before moving over to release the horses from their burden.

Sam Torrance had dismounted and slowly ambled over to the crest. Glancing down at the ferry, he called out. 'You two fellas had better get to pulling on that rope. I ain't swimming anywhere this day.'

Russ Decker sighed resignedly. He was pragmatic enough to realize that he was played out. He had tried and lost. This time! 'Take a hold of that cable,' he snarled at Naylor. 'Or I'll kick you so hard, you'll be wearing your ass for a hat.'

That man stared at him for a moment, before shuffling over to do as he was told. 'Gnun,' he non-sensically responded. The traumatic loss of his tongue seemed to have affected far more than just his speech.

The three men stood just below the crest of the banking and watched as the ferry slowly made its way towards them. With Torrance's tacit agreement, Taggart retained the big rifle. The marshal was quite obviously at the end of his tether and neither of them was fully convinced of Raoul's bona fides. And then of course there was the bank robber, who had more than demonstrated his belligerence.

'Just don't get to liking that long gun too much,' the lawman managed.

So it was that when the ferry finally arrived, the Winchester's temporary owner remarked to the tracker, 'I need to keep this gun on those two pus weasels, so I'd be much obliged if you'd round up the horses.'

Remarkably, Raoul acquiesced without argument and squelched back up to the crest. What he said next stunned the other two. 'Well that won't take long. There's only the one here, although I'll allow he's a fine looking animal.'

Despite the relentless pain in his skull, Marshal Torrance made the effort to join him. What he saw brought a grim smile to his haggard features. Sure enough, there remained only the one animal and for some incomprehensible reason it was his.

'Well I'll be. Only an Indian could have managed that, so there was one dogging my trail after all. He could have picked me off anytime he'd wanted, but he chose to wait and he's the richer for it.' The lawman shook his head in amazement, but then immediately regretted it. It seemed that there was just no accounting for the way an Indian thought!

CHAPTER THIRTEEN

There was no logical reason for it, but Raoul could feel eyes on him wherever he went. Guilt had a way of doing that to a man. His feet were sore and he wanted his boots. Yet there lay the rub. When he did recover them, he would need some time alone to transfer the thick wad of cash. And the cabin's other bed was now occupied by a Deputy US Marshal who, although sorely injured, still possessed eyes like gimlets.

The ferry, miraculously intact, had finally returned to its rightful place on the north bank. Its owner was nursing nothing more serious than a broken nose and some pretty impressive cuts and bruises, but it would be a long time before he got over the trauma of losing such a close companion to a pair of low-life traders.

In the absence of iron shackles, Russ Decker had his hands firmly tied behind his back. He stared into the middle distance, completely ignoring those around him. His immediate future would inevitably involve hard labour in a federal prison, but such a man never stayed down for long. It was just a crying shame that he had to have been thwarted by a half-breed!

The sunken keelboat's only survivor faced an uncertain future. Since nobody could ascertain his name and Sam Torrance was unaware of any paper out on him, Naylor was free to go, but his options were decidedly limited. Emptying bar room spittoons or begging for dimes would likely cover it.

Ben Exley had definitely experienced better outcomes to an assignment. His right hand was permanently disfigured and he had had agency dead to bury and read over. Compounding that was the presence of a federal officer, which meant that his organization was unable to claim credit for recovering the gold. The best that the Pinkertons could hope for was to charge a flat fee for the time and effort involved. All in all, he'd had a belly full of Taggart's Crossing. It was time to be gone. He glanced curiously over at his tracker. The 'breed had been acting squirrelly all day.

'There's nothing holding us here, Raoul,' he remarked. 'So unless you figure on riding barefoot, you'd best get your boots. We're leaving.'

That man stared back for a moment as though about to say something. Instead, Raoul finally turned and padded over to the cabin. His mind was turning summersaults in an effort to find an answer for his particular problem . . . but kept coming up short. As he entered the cabin, he was immediately aware of the marshal's eyes on him. God damn the son of a bitch, he thought to himself, Doesn't he ever sleep?'

Ignoring the law-dog, Raoul went straight to the other bed where the wounded Pinkerton had lain. His heart beat faster as he reached under and then steadied with relief as his searching hand settled on the leather boots. Retrieving them, he turned to leave. So far, so good.

'Nice paid of boots you got there, son,' the lawman abruptly remarked. It was the first time he had spoken to the tracker.

Raoul's heart raced. 'What does he know? Has he already found the cash?' Desperately, he attempted to maintain a normal demeanour. 'Why thanks, marshal,' he responded softly. 'I've had them for years. They fit like a glove.' With that, he made no attempt to put them on, but instead walked briskly to the door and out into the open.

What he found outside made his heart sink. Exley and the others were already mounted and just waiting on him. The massive ferryman was casually watching their departure, before making a start on some repairs to the ferry. With nothing else to do, Torrance's tightly bound prisoner was also idly observing events. Consequently all eyes were on the sweating tracker.

Raoul took a deep breath to steady himself and nonchalantly came to a halt. Dipping his toes into the left boot, he effortlessly pulled it on and then reached for the other. This time, as his foot slipped in, it quickly reached an obstruction. Curling his toes up, the man steeled himself for the inevitable pain and kicked down heavily against the ground. The thick wad of notes contracted only so far. Unable to conceal a grimace, he found that his heel was quite unable to settle in the rear of the boot.

'My foot must have swollen in the river,' he remarked by way of explanation. 'And these damned boots always were too tight anyway.' Hobbling towards his horse, he added, 'Happen they'll sort themselves out once I'm mounted.'

Exley stared at him askance, but remained silent. All he really wanted to do was return to Wichita and wash his hands of the whole business.

'That's a mighty bad limp you got there, fella,' Marshal Torrance remarked casually. 'How's about you shuck off that fancy boot.'

As Raoul froze, the lawman glanced meaningfully over at Taggart who cottoned on immediately. Everybody heard the distinctive sound of the big Winchester's lever action.

'Like I said,' Torrance continued. 'Lose the footwear.'

'What's the meaning of this,' demanded Exley, but nobody was listening. All eyes were riveted on his employee.

Very briefly, Raoul considered mounting up and making a break for it, but a bullet in the back held little appeal. His shoulders dropped in resignation and then he gratefully eased off the boot.

Torrance shuffled over to join him. 'Pick it up and give it to me,' he demanded.

With the boot in his hands, he up-ended and then shook it. A cold smile crossed his features as a pile of 'twenties' appeared at his feet. 'Look's like you thought to do a little private business,' he quipped.

What happened next took everyone by surprise, with the exception of Russ Decker, of course. 'Like hell, he is,' the outlaw spat out. 'He works for me. We made a deal.' He directed his next comments at Raoul. 'You stupid bastard. All you had to do was keep the cash hidden, but you couldn't even get that right!'

The Pinkerton tracker stared in stunned horror at his accuser and then it abruptly dawned on him what was happening. Turning to Ben Exley, he protested, 'Can't you see what he's trying to do. Yeah, I pocketed a few bills, but I've nothing to do with this low-life.'

Exley studied his employee closely as he began to put two and two together to make six. Chiefly, he recalled how Raoul had remained in the cabin whilst Decker had fled on the ferry. That suddenly smacked of connivance rather than self-preservation. And then there was the fact that he had been getting a little too big for his boots lately. Someone less serious might have seen the funny side of that thought, but as it was he merely replied, 'Nothing can alter the fact that you've betrayed my trust. I'm not sure whether you're in league with this man or not, but this is a federal matter, so it's out of my hands. I'll leave it to you, marshal.'

Torrance displayed no hesitation. 'Drop your

weapons and get over by the prisoner. You're under arrest. Way I see it, you've gone bad, but it'll be up to the judge to decide.'

As the tracker shuffled dejectedly over to join Decker, the outlaw couldn't restrain a chuckle. Things were starting to look up already!